WILLOW'S SECRETS

SALLY AVERY BERMANZOHN

Epigraph Books
Rhinebeck, New York

Cover drawing by Leola Bermanzohn

Book and cover design by Colin Rolfe

Paperback ISBN: 978-1-948796-96-5
eBook ISBN: 978-1-948796-97-2

Library of Congress Control Number: 2019916520

Epigraph Books
22 East Market Street, Suite 304
Rhinebeck, New York 12572
(845) 876-4861
epigraphps.com

To the memory of my parents,
Elfie Greene Avery and Roy Coleman Avery

Contents

CHAPTER 1

Cocoon

HOW DO I TELL THE story of my life? "Start at the beginning," my friends tell me as they recall memories when they were two or three years old. But I can't bring to mind anything when I was that young. My first memory is hiding behind Mama Rose's long skirts playing peek-a-boo with Grampa. Then Mama fell down. She said, "You knocked me over—you're a strong little five-year-old!"

That was a long time ago. I didn't know I had been "taken in" by Mama Rose and Grampa. I didn't know what had happened to my birth mother. Now I'm almost forty years old and I'm learning about my birth family. I am in a storytelling circle, learning how to tell the story of my life.

I remember Mama Rose's bed. I slept there when I was small. I often cried at night, and Mama had me sleep with her so she could comfort me. We lived in the woods, and sometimes we heard coyotes howl. They scared me. Mama said the coyotes were just talking to each other—they wouldn't hurt us.

One dark night, Mama and I were both fast asleep. Suddenly, there was loud knocking at the front door: *Knock, Knock, Knock!* I slipped out of bed and ran into the living room to see what was happening. I saw Grampa in his nightshirt grabbing his double-barreled shotgun off the hooks high on the living room wall. Then Grampa shoved his foot hard on the front door to open it fast and pointed the gun at the person who was knocking.

I never saw who was there, because Mama pulled me back in her bedroom. "Don't you ever run out of this room if you hear a noise in the night!" she scolded me. "It is Grampa's job to protect us, and he can't do it if you're running around!" I cried because I was scared, and then Mama hugged me. "You're almost too big for lullabies," Mama said, and it was true. But she sang one anyway, and I fell asleep.

The next morning, Grampa told me that when he heard the knocking he mustered his gun, in case someone was intending to harm us. But the man at the door was just a traveler looking for a place to sleep with a roof over his head. Grampa pointed to the shacks across the road that were for travelers.

We lived in the hill country of northern Alabama on a small farm. Usually it was just me, Mama, and Grampa. During the summer and Christmas, my big brother Thomas stayed with us. Most of the time, Thomas lived with relatives down in Birmingham, where he went to school.

I remember celebrating my sixth birthday. Mama baked a cake, and she and Grampa sang "Happy Birthday, dear Willow" to me. Grampa and Mama made a bedroom in the pantry right off the kitchen just for me. It had a small window that looked out to the backyard where I could watch the moon at night. I heard noises of all shapes and sizes. Most of them were not worth fretting over—but not all. Grampa's soldierly response to a knock at the door gave me the notion that some noises might be signs of danger.

I have lots of memories of after I turned six—like going to the barn with Grampa every morning to feed our cow and the chickens, cats, donkey, and Grampa's Palomino horse, whose name was Pal. I remember Mama cooking. She loved her cast iron skillet more than anything in the world. Sometimes I would sneak pieces of her cornbread when she wasn't looking.

I remember my grandmother, who did not like me. I didn't like her either. When I came near her, she told me, "Run along, Sister Daisy." My name was not Daisy, so I looked around to see who she was talking to. I puzzled over and pondered this mystery for months but was afraid to ask her. That question was answered on Christmas, when Thomas was home. Grandmother said to him, "Run along, Sister Daisy." Mystery solved! Every kid was Sister Daisy to Grandmother.

Grandmother was old and sick, and didn't like young children bothering her. I learned to stay away from her. She couldn't walk, so Mama pushed her around in an old wooden wheelchair. The wheelchair squeaked, and when I heard it I got out of the way. Then Grandmother got so sick she stayed in bed all the time. Then she died.

Mama and Grampa were very sad when Grandmother died. The minister came, and they buried her in our family cemetery, right next to our house. I remember watching them dig up the dirt for her grave. I played in that soft, good-smelling dirt while they prayed and carried on.

Grampa always called Mama *Mama Rose*, even though she was his daughter. Her name was Rose. Mama called her father Papa, and I called him Grampa. When

I was young, I thought that Mama was my mother and Grampa was my grandfather. When I was older, Mama told me that I had a different birth mother who died when I was very little. After my birth mother died, Mama and Grampa took me in and raised me. Mama said she didn't want to tell me this sad story, but I asked so many questions. I wanted to know everything.

Mama and Grampa were not sure when I was born. Was it 1866, or 1867, or 1868? It was one of those hard, starving years after the Civil War. They simply took me in and told everyone I was Mama's child. As I grew, Mama and Grampa wanted to celebrate my birthday, so they chose March 1, 1867. Every year on that date, Mama baked a cake and we celebrated.

Looking back, I realize how patient Mama and Grampa were with me. I was full of energy and always asking questions. I loved Mama, but we were very different. She stayed in the house, and I liked to be outside. She liked to cook, and I liked to dig in the dirt. When she wasn't cooking, Mama sat in the living room and sewed. I never sat for long. When I asked Mama questions, she usually ignored me. Sometimes she looked so unhappy, and I felt like she was looking right through me. When Mama got sad, I got sad. I wanted to fly away.

I loved Grampa because he was fun and taught me things. He told me stories about when he was a boy. He said his best friends were Chickasaw Indian boys who lived here. That was a long time ago, when this was Chickasaw Country, before the Americans forced the Indians to leave their home.

Grampa listened to my questions and, most of the time, he answered them. If I asked a hard question, he would take

4

hours—or days—before responding to me. When I complained about him taking too long, he told me to be patient.

Grampa wanted to teach me to read, and he got angry at me when I couldn't sit still. When he was angry, or Mama was sad, I went to my secret hideout. I found this hideout one day when I was exploring the hill behind our cornfield—way back behind our house. I saw a rocky ledge that jutted out near the top of the hill. The hill under the ledge was too steep for me to climb, so I walked around to the side of the hill where the slope was not so steep. I climbed through the woods up to the hilltop and found a way out onto the ledge. There I could sit on the rocks, feel the wind, and imagine I was flying. Up, up, away from Mama and Grampa—I felt like I was up there with the birds.

"Where do you go," asked Grampa, "when you disappear for hours at a time?" We were sitting in the kitchen while Mama fixed vittles.

"To my secret hideout," I told him. "No one knows where it is. I want to live there."

When it came to food, Mama could be loud and opinionated. "Hogwash!" she declared about my idea of living in my hideout. "How will you eat?"

"I will come here for meals."

"Not in this house." she said. "You have to help around here if you want to eat." "How will you sleep?" asked Grampa with respect, or maybe skepticism.

"I will make a soft bed out of leaves."

"How will you stop the bears and snakes from hurting you?" he asked, mocking me in his tone of wonder.

"Oh." I hadn't thought about that.

"You got it all figured out," muttered Grampa, "except for eating and staying safe."

One day, after chores I went to my hideout and stayed for hours. It rained, and I got cold, but I stayed anyway. Then I got hungry and came home.

Mama and Grampa were angry at me. "I rang the cow bell and you didn't come. We waited dinner for you," Mama said. Grampa sent me to bed without supper. But later, when Grampa wasn't looking, Mama brought soup and bread to my bedroom.

"Thank you, Mama," I said. The soup tasted great, and I knew Mama loved me.

The next day, Grampa told me that he and Mama had written down rules that I had to follow to eat and sleep in this house. I still remember them, because Grampa read those rules to me over and over. Years later, when I finally learned how to write sentences, he made me copy the rules and tape them to my bedroom door.

RULES OF THIS HOUSE

1. Be in the house before meals to set the table.
2. Clean up after meals. Wash and dry dishes, and put them away.
3. Do your chores—feed the chickens, weed the cornfield and vegetable garden.
4. Work with all of us during the planting and the harvest.
5. Always be home before it gets dark.
6. Come home immediately whenever you hear Mama's cowbell.
7. Respect your mother and grandfather.

Years later, as an adult, I appreciated Mama and Grampa more than I can say. They loved me, and they were strict but patient. They never hit or hurt me. Those rules were good ones.

We lived in the country, surrounded by hills and woods and meadows. No one lived near us except for the family who lived next door. They were the Henrys: Miz Mildred and her husband, Mr. Henry, and their daughter Molly. They were our best friends. Mama and Miz Mildred grew up together, and they each married good men. Miz Mildred had a girl child she named Molly, and Mama had me. Molly and I were best friends, even though Molly was six years older than me. I didn't realize until years later that Molly and her folks were "colored."

Mama told me that Molly's family lived "a skip and a jump" from our house. But Molly taught me how to count, and I counted the space between our houses. It took me twenty-seven skips. And if I jumped, it took thirty-two jumps. Mama was seldom wrong, but I counted the jumps. I decided not to argue with Mama over it.

Molly taught me lots of things, especially about plants and animals. One summer day, she showed me a twig on a bush that had a hard, dark thing on it. I thought the dark thing was a dry leaf. "It's not a leaf," said Molly. "It's a cocoon."

"What's a cocoon?" I asked her.

"It's a safe place for a tiny little creature. We will watch this twig every day, to see what happens to the cocoon."

We checked the cocoon every day. One morning, I saw something trying to struggle out of it. I ran to get Molly, and we both sat there watching it. Then a beautiful butterfly crawled out of the cocoon. The butterfly sat near the cocoon for a while. "It's drying out its wings," said Molly. Then it gracefully flew away to Mama's flower bed.

CHAPTER 2

The Same Underneath

BOTH MOLLY'S FAMILY AND MY family were poor.
My family owned twenty acres of land, and the
Henrys also owned twenty acres right next to us.
Having land meant we could grow our own food. Our
two families shared the barn that housed our animals, the
woodshed where we stored wood, and the well that provided us with good drinking water. Our families worked
together to plant and harvest the cornfields.

Fall was always the busiest time of the year, because
that's when we harvested and preserved most of our
crops. We had a routine. Mama always cooked us a big
breakfast of scrambled eggs, grits, and cornbread, then
our two families sat around our big living room table to
eat. On the first morning of the harvest, Grampa would
say, "We are two small families, but together we have
five people who can work the harvest while Mama Rose
cooks the meals for us."

Then Mr. Henry, winking at Molly and me, said, "Who
needs sons? We don't—because we have such strong
hard-working daughters."

"Where shall we start, Mr. Henry?" Grampa said. This
was a joke, because we always started in the Henrys' cornfield. Their cornfield was in the shade in the early morning,

and our cornfield was shaded in the late afternoon. Grampa said, "The more work you can do in the shade, the better."

We worked in teams. One team was Miz Mildred and her husband Mr. Henry. Another was Molly and me. Grampa worked by himself. As we walked down the rows of corn, we pulled off all the big ripe cobs and left the smaller cobs on the stalk. We would harvest those cobs a week or so later when they were ripe. And we always left some cobs for the crows and critters.

By midmorning, we were working in the hot sun. When Mama rang the cowbell for lunch, we were always relieved. We stopped by our pond, where we cooled off by splashing our sweaty faces and bodies.

Mama had a good lunch ready on the picnic table under the shade of the big oak tree. She fixed deviled eggs one day, potato salad the next, and always cornbread and cold tea. Before we ate lunch, Mama gave the blessing, "Thank you, God, for this beautiful land that provides us with our food. In Jesus' name, Amen." Then we would eat and relax for a while. Often the grownups stayed at the table, talking, while Molly and I would lie under the willow tree and fall asleep.

I remember one day when Mr. Henry said something that kept me at the picnic table. He said, "The way we work together reminds me of the ways of the Choctaw Indians. Each family would have their own kitchen garden. And the village had big community fields of corn, squash, pumpkins, beans, and sunflowers. The whole village worked together to harvest the big fields—just like we do here."

Mr. Henry sighed, "In a way, our two families are like a little Choctaw village."

"Are you an Indian, Mr. Henry?" I asked him. I had heard Grampa talk about the Chickasaw Indians who used to live here. But, as far as I knew, I had never met an Indian.

"Can you keep a secret?" Mr. Henry said, glancing at me with a serious look.

"Yes," I answered.

"Okay, then," whispered Mr. Henry. "My mother was a Choctaw Indian and my father was African. "I will tell you my story if you promise to keep it secret and never tell anyone."

I nodded my head, saying, "I'm good at keeping secrets."

"When I was young," Mr. Henry said, "the government soldiers rounded up the Choctaws and the other Indian tribes here in the South and forced them to go west to Indian Territory. No one wanted to leave their homeland, but the soldiers had lots of guns.

"I was still little," Mr. Henry continued, his face saddened. "My cousin took me with him to the city of Mobile. I was away from my mother when the soldiers came. I never saw her again.

"After that, I couldn't be a Choctaw any more, even though I was born and raised Choctaw. Ever since that Indian Removal Law, being an Indian is *illegal* here in the South. If I said I was Choctaw, they could send me out west, so I became a colored man of African descent."

While Mr. Henry was talking, I looked at each one of us. Mr. Henry's wife Mildred had dark brown skin. Mr. Henry was also brown, but lighter than his wife. Molly's color was in-between her parents. Then I looked at Grampa. He always wore a hat, and his face stayed beige, but his arms were very tan from working in the sun.

10

Then I looked at my own brown arms and saw that my skin was much darker than Grampa's, but lighter than Mr. Henry's. Mama's skin was the lightest of all, because she hardly ever left the house.

A few days later, when I was alone with Grampa, I talked to him about the skin colors of our two families. Grampa said, "You make some interesting observations. But many folks see it differently. They consider you, me, and Mama to be 'white,' and Molly, Mildred, and Henry to be 'colored.'"

"Why?" I asked.

"Because the Alabama government believes in the 'separation of the races.' In fact, the whole South, and much of the rest of this country, tries to separate people by color. They make laws about it."

"That doesn't make sense," I said.

"You're right," Grampa said. "We are all the same underneath our different skins. And the way we work and live with the Henrys shows that people can get along if they want to."

I was glad that we were close friends with the Henrys, helping each other out so we all could eat. We farmed together and gathered wood together to make the fires that kept us warm all winter. Being different colors did not matter at all. We worked hard but also had time to play, and talk, and learn.

Mr. and Mrs. Henry were like second parents to me. In the summer, it always got real hot, and Molly and I were always trying to cool off. One day, we were playing at the well our families shared. It was very hot, and we were splashing each other with the cold well water that comes from down deep in the earth. That water felt good!

Suddenly Miz Mildred came running out of her house, yelling at us, *"If you don't stop wasting our well water, I'm gonna take my strap to your behinds!"*

It was the first time I had ever hear Miz Mildred raise her voice. I ran away from her towards my house and almost bumped into Mama, who was headed out the door to see what the commotion was about.

"Molly and I were hot, and we were just cooling off like we do at the pond," I explained to Mama.

Mama grabbed my arm, "Do you drink pond water?"

"No," I answered. "Pond water is dirty."

"If our well water runs dry—which can happen in this dry hot weather—then we will have to drink pond water." Mama was angry, and she sounded just like Miz Mildred. She was holding my arm tight, and it hurt.

"You can swim and play in the pond all you want," Mama said. "But well water is only for drinking and cooking. Do you understand me?"

When Grampa came home that day, Mama told him about the well. Then he said to me, "We will whip you if you ever waste our drinking water again."

Molly's parents told her the same thing. That was the only time Molly and I were ever threatened with a whipping. Years later, I realized that she and I were lucky to have parents who talked to us, rather than beat us.

CHAPTER 3

The Floozy

T HE WINTER I WAS FIVE, Grandmother got real sick. Mama spent most of her time taking care of her, and I spent a lot of time at Molly's house staying out of the way. Then Grandmother died. Mama told me she was a wonderful mother, and Grampa told me she was a wonderful wife. They talked about her all the time. I learned real quick not to roll my eyes.

That summer, my brother Thomas came home from Birmingham, where he was in school. As usual, he stayed with us all summer. Grampa was happy to have Thomas around. He took Thomas on trips *just for men folk*, even though Thomas was only a small, skinny eleven-year- old. They traveled to Mississippi in Grampa's buggy pulled by Pal, and they had a good time. Grampa explained to me that after his wife died he needed to make new friends and have fun. Mama Rose disapproved, saying Grampa was wasting money.

At the end of the summer, Thomas went back to school in Birmingham. But Grampa kept going on trips down to Mississippi, telling us he had met new people and was enjoying life.

That fall, Grampa came home and said he had a surprise for us. "I met a young lady, and we're going to get married." Then he added, "She's a young one, but I do love her."

Next time he came back from Mississippi, he told us that he had gotten married! He was going to bring his new wife, Annabelle, up to meet us. A few weeks later, he showed up with his bride Annabelle, who had blue eyes and blond ringlets. They moved into Grampa's bedroom.

Molly hung out at our house, fascinated with Annabelle. Molly stared at Mama, who was watching Annabelle. Molly told me, "If looks could kill, Annabelle and your Grampa would be dead."

Mama never liked Annabelle. She spent a lot of time at the Henrys' house, where Mama complained to Miz Mildred on and on about Annabelle. "That floozy is young enough to be my father's *granddaughter*!" Molly and I sat there listening to every word.

Then Mama muttered to Miz Mildred, "And it looks like she's already got a bun in the oven."

I whispered to Molly, "What's a bun in the oven? When can we eat it?" Molly shushed me with her finger and motioned to me to follow her. Outside, Molly told me that it meant that Grampa's new wife was going to have a baby.

That Christmas, when Thomas came from Birmingham to visit, Annabelle had a belly as big as a cantaloupe. Even with her loose-fitting clothing, Annabelle's *bun* was showing.

When Grampa took Annabelle out to dinner with the horse and buggy, Mama told me and Thomas, "Your Grampa is an old fool. He's spending a heap of money on her. He's likely to bring shame on our family's good name."

I didn't understand what Mama meant. Grampa seemed happy, and Annabelle was nice. Why was Mama was so upset?

Mama had a sideboard in our living room, which she told me was her one nice piece of furniture, from the old days when the family was well off. It was made of fine oak, with glass door cabinets above a countertop and more cabinets below. I could see Mama's good china through the glass doors, and Mama's other nice things were in the cabinets below. I was forbidden to touch anything near that sideboard.

One day, I saw Annabelle standing next to the side-board, dreamily touching it and looking at Mama's fine china. She quietly opened a glass door and took out one of Mama's delicate tea cups, pretending to sip tea out of it.

I coughed, and Annabelle saw me, quickly putting the tea cup back. "Why it's little Willow," she said, giving me a charming smile.

"Mama doesn't let anyone touch her china," I said sternly. "Oh," Annabelle responded, "I would never hurt anything." "Annabelle, are you gonna have a baby?" I asked her.

"Yes, I am," she replied, touching her growing belly. "Is Grampa the daddy?"

"Yes, he is." Annabelle looked at me seriously. "We *are* married, you know." "Will the baby be my sister?" I asked.

"Well, ah … I don't rightly know," stammered Annabelle. I watched her standing there, thinking. Finally, she said to me, "Let's just call her 'baby.'"

After Christmas, Grampa took Annabelle back to Mississippi because she wanted to be with her mother when the baby was born. Her baby boy came in February.

In April, Grampa went down to Mississippi and brought his new wife and child home. I liked Annabelle and had fun playing with the baby, who was named Little Jack, after Grampa.

Mama said Grampa was an idiot—behind his back. She called Annabelle a floozy.

"What's a floozy?" I asked Mama.

"A floozy is a no-account, low-class woman who tries to take advantage of an old fool like your grandfather," she muttered. She was angry.

I didn't know whether to believe Mama or Grampa. Was Annabelle a *floozy*, or as Grampa described her, *a sweet young thing*?

Turned out Mama was right—Grampa's new wife was a floozy! One night that summer, Annabelle disappeared, baby and all. Grampa was upset and worried that she'd been kidnapped.

Then Grampa discovered that our family's precious items had been stolen the same night that Annabelle disappeared. Grampa had buried those valuables in an iron safe-box in our woods during the Civil War to keep the soldiers from robbing them from our house. During the hard times after the war, Grampa had used some of those valuables to pay our land taxes.

When Mama heard that the valuables were gone, she yelled at Grampa, "You boob! She hoodwinked you. I bet that baby wasn't even yours." It was the only time I heard Mama raise her voice to her father.

Grampa got on his horse and rode down to Mississippi to try to find Annabelle. People down there told Grampa that Annabelle and her mother had "gone west." Mama told me, "Once people go west, there's no way to find them, 'cause the West is huge and wild." She paused, wiped her brow, and added, "Your Grampa is the laughingstock of Alabama."

Even worse than being embarrassed, we were suddenly very poor. Mama explained to me that we needed to make enough money every year to pay our land taxes, as well as eat. If we didn't pay our taxes, the government would take our land away from us. "Now we have only the crops we raise on our farm," Mama said, "What will happen if there's a big storm, or drought, and all our crops get ruined? Then we'll have nothing to eat and no money to pay taxes."

After Grampa got back from Mississippi, Mama was so furious that she stopped talking to Grampa. She packed her suitcase and went to stay with Aunt Daisy, her sister who lived down the road.

Without Mama's cooking, we had only makeshift meals. Grampa went to the grocery store and bought a big burlap bag full of what people called "goober peas." He said they were used to feed livestock, but during the war hungry soldiers ate them. Grampa said they were good once they were boiled in water. He filled my hands with them and then sang, "Peas, peas, peas, peas—eatin' goober peas. Goodness, how delicious—eatin' goober peas!"

I took one and put it in my mouth. "Yuck!" I spitted it out. Grampa picked up the thing from the floor, and cracked open the shell, and out came this little goober pea. He rubbed his stomach and sang, "goodness, how delicious—eatin' goober peas!" Then Grampa boiled the goober peas for us.

That night the Henrys invited us over for dinner, and Grampa told them about the goober peas. Miz Mildred laughed, "Some baby sitter you are!" I laughed too. Then I told Miz Mildred that I wasn't a baby and that I liked Grampa showing me grownup stuff. And I got to like goober peas, which we ate nearly every day.

Finally, Mama came back home. That night, after I was sent to bed I overheard Mama talking to Grampa. "I forgive you," she told him, "because it is the Christian thing to do. You've always been a good father to me and you were a good husband to my mother." Then she paused and added, "I pray you have learned your lesson about floozies." Grampa said nothing.

The next morning, Mama Rose told me why she forgave Grampa. And she added a lesson just for me: "Men can be fools," she said. "Mark my words."

We grew enough food to eat that year, but little more than that. To pay our land taxes Grampa had to sell his buggy and his beautiful horse Pal. I missed Pal. We had to walk everywhere. After Annabelle ran away, things gradually calmed down in our house. And I stopped thinking about the floozy.

CHAPTER 4

Bean Seeds
and Pollywogs

O NE FALL DAY, MAMA AND I were in front of
our house, pruning her rosebush. "Rose" is a
family name, my grandmother's name was Rose,
and so was my mama's name. The big rosebush next to
our front porch was precious to Mama Rose because it
had been a gift from her husband before he died in the
war. Mama cut the dead twigs and faded blossoms off
the bush and gently handed them to me to put in a basket. I was small then and had to be careful so the thorns
wouldn't scratch me.

Mama and I watched as an old woman walked up the
road into our yard, someone I had never seen before.

"Who's that?" I asked Mama. She didn't answer me.
Instead, Mama waved to the old woman like she knew
her. "Good morning," said Mama.

"Good morning, Rose. Good morning, Willow," the
old woman said. Her face was full of wrinkles and
browned by the sun. Her grey and black hair hung in
long braids. She wore an old skirt, a loose-fitting blouse,
and old leather slippers on her feet.

"Willow," Mama nudged me, "say hello." "Hello, I'm Willow," I said.

"I know you're Willow," said the old woman, smiling at me.

Mama pointed to the big oak tree on the side of our house. "Willow, take Auntie to the bench under the tree. It is warm there in the sun. You both have a seat out there, and I will bring out tea and biscuits for us."

The old woman and I walked over and sat on the bench under the oak while Mama puttered in the kitchen. I couldn't take my eyes off the old woman, feeling that, somehow, I knew her.

Mama must know her, because Mama would never leave me alone with a stranger.

The old woman reached into her pocket and brought out some bean seeds. "Save these in a dry place," she told me, "And next spring you can plant them in your garden."

After we had tea, Mama and I showed her around the farm. We showed her our cornfield, the Henrys' cornfield, our vegetable garden, Grampa's sweet potato patch, and my little garden next to the sweet potatoes.

"This is a great spot for you to plant those bean seeds," the old woman said to me.

I pulled the seeds out of my pocket and showed them to Mama. She said, "We will store them in a dry place and plant them next spring."

Then the old woman looked at the sky and said, "The sun is my clock, and the sun's telling me it's time to leave now. I've got a long walk home."

At dinner that night, I asked Mama and Grampa about the old woman.

"You don't remember her visiting last year?" Mama asked. "She came to see you last year, and you hid behind me," Mama said, laughing.

I asked, "Does she walk around visiting small girls?" Grampa and Mama looked at each other. Then Grampa said, "She is your special person. She knows plants, and she wants to teach you."

"Call her Auntie," said Mama. "She likes to visit once a year, in the fall after the harvest and before the frost."

Grampa wanted to teach me to read. Our village did not have a schoolhouse, because it had been burned down during the Civil War. Molly and my big brother Thomas learned to read because my Grampa taught them, right here in this house. They were both smart, and they worked hard. They learned how to read books and newspapers.

When I was six, Grampa told me that I was old enough to learn how to read and that he would teach me with Molly's help. One spring morning at breakfast, Grampa said to me, "After breakfast, I want you to run next door and invite Molly to come over. We need to talk about giving you some reading lessons."

I finished my porridge and ran outside to find Molly. "Hi there, Willow," said Molly's mama when I knocked on her door. "If you're looking for Molly, she's down at the pond."

"Thank you!" I called and ran down the path that went through Molly's family's cornfield and through the woods. I kept running until I reached the pond down in the hollow beyond the trees.

There I found Molly staring into the water. Molly was much older and bigger than me. "Come quick Willow," she whispered, "Look what we got in our pond."

"Oh—look at the fishies," I said, looking at lots of little fishies, swimming, side by side, all in the same direction.

"They're *not* fishies," declared Molly. "Yes, they *are* fishies!" I said.

"Nope. They are *pollywogs*. They are baby frogs."

"Look like fishies to me. They're swimming with tails like fish do. Frogs don't have tails. Frogs have big hopping legs."

"Bet you a nickel they're baby frogs," said Molly. "I can't make a bet 'cause I don't have a nickel."

"No one 'round here has a nickel. Forget the bet. We'll watch them every day," said Molly, "and you will see little tiny frog legs grow and grow—and their tails will get smaller and smaller. Then you will see that they are pollywogs becoming frogs."

"I don't think so."

"Just wait—I know what I'm talking about." Molly smiled confidently, patting the air with both her hands as if to say "calm down, child!"

The sun felt hot. There were big, flat sunning rocks next to the pond, and Molly stretched out on hers, which was the biggest one. I sat down on mine, which was smaller than Molly's 'cause Molly was big and I was small. I liked my rock because I could lie on it and put my feet in the pond at the same time. We lay there under the cottonwood tree, each thinking her own thoughts.

Then Molly told me she was thinking about her next birthday, which was a long way off. "I know what I want for my birthday," she whispered. "I want to go to Birmingham and spend a week with my cousins."

When Molly mentioned Birmingham, it made me think about my brother Thomas, who was going to school in

Birmingham. I was curious about Thomas. He was the same age as Molly, and Grampa had taught them both to read. I asked Molly what Thomas was like when he was little like me.

"Oh, Thomas?" Molly said, "He's always been quiet, kept to himself. But he was a good learner. Almost good as me."

"Why doesn't he come up here more often to visit?"

"I can't rightly say. Maybe it's 'cause the deaths in your family made your Mama so sad. I don't think Thomas likes that sadness. I know something else about Thomas— he don't like to farm."

We lay there sunning. Then we heard Molly's mama calling her, "Molly, time for chores."

We got up. Molly said, "Goodbye pollywogs!"

I said, "Goodbye fishies!" Then we headed back up the path, walking slowly because it had gotten hot. Molly went to her house, and I went to mine.

As the kitchen door shut behind me, Grampa asked, "When is Molly coming over to talk about reading lessons?"

"Oh Grampa—I forgot about the lessons! Molly showed me these fish she said were pollywogs, and we got to talking about them, and..."

"Willow, stop!" grumbled Grampa. "I don't care about pollywogs. I care about you learning to read. *You can't seem to sit still long enough to learn anything!*"

"I'm sorry, Grampa. Let me go back over there and give Molly your message." And that's what I did.

That night after supper, Molly came over. We set up what Grampa called *lesson plans*. Molly had already taught me the "ABC Song." Next she was going to teach me to write all the letters—all twenty-six of them. Grampa had tried to teach me to write the letters with a pencil. But I couldn't do it. My hand just couldn't hang on to a pencil.

Molly had an idea, which she told me about when Grampa was not around. She would teach me to write the ABCs with a stick in the mud next to the pond. Then we could watch the pollywogs (if she was right), or fishies (if I was right). And that's what we did. I learned to write letters in the mud. "You're a quick study," Molly told me.

Then one day it rained, and we sat in Molly's house at the eating table, and Molly handed me paper and a pencil. To my surprise, I could write my ABCs with a pencil on a paper. I learned to make each letter in the mud with a stick, then with a pencil on paper in the house. I learned to write *all* my letters. Grampa was proud of my progress.

Meanwhile, Molly and I watched the pollywogs. Molly was right—they did slowly turn into frogs, just the way she said. Everyday their tiny forelegs and hind legs got a little bigger and their tails got smaller. Every day there were fewer of them. "Where are the pollywogs going?" I asked Molly.

"Hawks and snakes are eating some of them," said Molly quietly, almost whispering, as if it were a secret.

"Oh," I said. "Poor little pollywogs. They need protection!" Then I thought that I was lucky to have Grampa and Mama to keep me safe as my legs got bigger and stronger day by day—just like the pollywogs. Right then, I decided to be a fast runner when I got big, fast enough to outrun bears and snakes.

That fall, Auntie visited me again. I showed her my garden with the beans stalks I grew from her seeds. Mama cooked those beans, and they were delicious. Auntie gave me pumpkin seeds and sunflower seeds to plant in the springtime. Mama and I stored them, safe and dry, in our pantry. In the spring, when the earth got warm, I planted those seeds in my garden.

One year, Auntie gave me seedlings as well as seeds. The seedlings were little mint and sage plants that had just sprouted from their seeds. We planted them right away in my garden because, Auntie explained, "they need to get settled before the frost." When the frost came weeks later, I got upset because it looked like the mint and the sage were dead. But in the spring a miracle happened. Little green shoots came back up through the warm earth, and they grew and grew all summer.

The mint plants had babies, and every year there were more of them, spreading everywhere. Some of them went into Grampa's sweet potatoes, and he had to pull them up so they wouldn't smother his precious sweet potatoes. But most of the mint was in a good spot for spreading, and Mama and I made mint tea all year long. We also made mint jelly, which Mama and I love to this day.

Looking back on my early years, I felt like I lived in a cocoon with my Mama Rose and Grampa, and with my best friend Molly and her parents. And I had the nice old woman who visited me every fall and taught me about plants. How well protected I was from the meanness of the outside world.

But then the world started to cross over into my life. The village began to build a new one-room schoolhouse.

CHAPTER 5

Breaking Ground

During the summer when I was seven, Grampa talked about the plan to build a new schoolhouse in Pine Hill, the village closest to our farm. It was 1874, and there had been no school anywhere near here because, during the Civil War, the Yankees had burned down the old schoolhouse. "That was ten years ago," Grampa told me. "You'd think people would have rebuilt the schoolhouse by now."

A few weeks later, Grampa came home with a flyer that he read:

Groundbreaking Ceremony
for the New Pine Hill Public School
August 15 at 9:00 a.m.
Lot between Church and Grocery Store
Everyone invited

Grampa said, "It's important for us to go." The morning of the groundbreaking, Grampa pounded on my bedroom door. "Willow—time to rise and shine! We can't be late for the ceremony."

I heard Grampa and Mama bickering in the kitchen, right next to my bedroom. Mama said, "I am *not* going to the groundbreaking!"

"Come on, Rose," Grampa grumbled. "You got to show yourself in the village. Don't be a stick-in-the-mud. You can't just hide in this house. It's important to support the school."

Mama raised her voice, "I don't want to 'show myself!' Too many no-count people around here." Then she whispered, "One of those men killed my husband."

I wondered what Mama was talking about. As she was speaking, I opened my bedroom door and stepped into the noisy kitchen. Grampa and Mama stopped arguing and looked at me.

"Our little school girl!" exclaimed Grampa.

"Not so fast," muttered Mama. "They got to build that schoolhouse first. No telling how long that'll take."

Grampa didn't say anything.

After breakfast I put on my Sunday-go-to-meeting dress that Mama had sewed me. Grampa put on his good shirt and his indoor pants with the good suspenders. We set out for the spot where the school would be built. It was a long walk from our house.

"Why is it taking folks so long to build a one-room schoolhouse?" I asked Grampa as we headed down the road.

Grampa kept walking and didn't answer, so I asked him again.

"You ask an important question, Willow," he said. "And I'm thinking about how to explain it."

Finally, he stopped walking, turned to look at me, and said, "The Civil War was hard on lots of folks—fear, hunger, death, lots of suffering. Many folks are still mourning their loved ones who died."

Grampa took a deep breath. "That war divided the people around here, Confederates against Unionists. A bunch of men, including me, didn't want to fight for the South. We didn't want to risk getting killed so that rich plantation owners could keep their slaves. We were Unionists, hoping the Yankees would win the war real quick. But the Civil War dragged on and on for four years. Lots of young men on both sides died in the fighting—including my only son, Robert. He was a fine boy, just sixteen years old."

Grampa took out his handkerchief and wiped his eyes. "That was years ago, but folks still blame their own suffering on their neighbors who were on the other side of the war. That's why this community is having a hard time building a school to teach our children."

Grampa started walking again—fast because he didn't want to be late. But I still had questions. "Is that why Mama looks so sad?" I asked.

"Yes," said Grampa as he kept walking. "Your Mama's husband Thomas was murdered just as the war started. It was a terrible tragedy for her. Mama Rose and I still mourn Robert and Thomas." Grampa looked so sad.

"Poor Grampa, poor Mama," I thought.

We came to the clearing where they planned to build the school. Several men came over and shook my Grampa's hand. One walked with crutches because his foot was missing. He was very happy to see Grampa.

There was a chalk line drawn on the ground that outlined where the four sides of the schoolhouse would be. Papa and I stood on one side of the chalk line with the man on crutches and some men, women, and children. Across from us, on the other side of the chalk square, another group of people stood talking with each other, their kids playing around. As we walked up, I saw some of those people scowl at us. I figured they must be the ones on the other side of the war.

Then the young preacher, wearing black pants and a black shirt with a white collar, stepped into the middle of the chalk square. He raised his hands, and everyone got quiet.

"We are gathered together here," the preacher began, "to rebuild the Pine Hill Public School, to educate the children of this community. It will take efforts from all parts of this village." The preacher paused and looked at each person.

"All of us," he continued, "need to forgive each other and get beyond the suffering of the past. We must move forward together into the future." He paused and then said, "God bless the rebuilding of this school. In the name of God, the Father, and Jesus Christ, Amen."

Then the preacher introduced a heavyset man wearing a new suit and tie. Grampa whispered to me, "That's the Alabama government man."

The government man talked about what a good spot this was to build the school, right between the church and the grocery store, and across from the field where children play and families had picnics.

The government man said, "You as a village will work together to build this school. When you are done, the State of Alabama will provide you with a schoolteacher. This school will be run according to the *laws* and *customs* of the State of Alabama."

Grampa leaned over and whispered to me, "That means it will be a *white-only* school." I didn't know what he meant, and tugged at his shirt sleeve to ask, but he ignored me. "Will everyone have to wear white clothes?"

I wondered, looking around at the people. Only a few had white clothes on. My dress was half white and half colored flowers. I wondered what colors had to do with going to school to learn stuff.

Next a young man named Luke stepped forward. Unlike the preacher and the government man, Luke wore old overalls and looked like he lived here. "Building this schoolhouse is going to take all of us working together," he said. Then he handed out shovels to some of the men, including my grandfather. I noticed that he gave half of the shovels to the men on our side of the chalk square, and the other shovels to the men on the other side.

As the men took their shovels and stepped into the square, the adults started talking to each other and the kids started chasing each other. With his back to me, Grampa dug up some dirt. I watched his back.

Suddenly a big boy ran into me. As he bumped me, he muttered, "*This school is white only. It ain't for you!*"

I didn't know who the boy was talking to. Then, right behind him, another boy pushed me, knocking me to my knees. He hissed, "*No Indians allowed!*"

I scrambled to get back up on my feet. I was scared. They were big. Why were they hurting me? I hadn't done anything to them. I'd never even seen them before.

Then a third boy ran by me, pushed me, and whispered in my ear, "*You're dead!*" Then he ran off.

I struggled to keep from falling again. I saw Grampa's back just a few feet in front of me. He was leaning on his shovel, talking to his friend. I ran up to him, and he put his arm around my shoulders and kept talking to his friend. My heart was pounding—those boys scared me!

30

But I knew they would not hurt me as long as my Grampa had his arm around me.

I looked across the chalk square and saw those three rowdy boys, still laughing and roughhousing. Holding onto my Grampa, I watched them. No one seemed to notice that they had pushed me down.

Then the men put down their shovels. They said good-bye to each other and left. With his arm still on my shoulders, Grampa and I started towards our house. I looked back over my shoulder and saw those mean boys walking off with their father in the opposite direction. Grampa and I walked home. I said nothing.

When we got home, I quickly changed into my old clothes. I wanted to be outside and didn't feel hungry for lunch. I ran through the woods behind our house, past the cornfield to the hill. I climbed up the side of the hill to my secret hideout. Sitting there on the rock ledge, I could see our farm and the Henrys' farm. It was breezy up there, and I loved the wind.

"I wish I could live up here with the wind," I thought, "far away from those mean boys." I talked out loud to myself. "I'm tough—I can run fast!" But those boys had scared me. I didn't want to tell Grampa because he would tell Mama. Then she would get upset and sad. I felt tired, and I dozed up there in my hideout. Then Mama's cow-bell woke me up. She was calling me home to do chores.

At supper that night, I didn't know what to say, so I didn't say anything. Grampa told Mama about the groundbreaking. I asked Grampa, "Why did you all stop shoveling? There's lots more ground to dig."

"It was just a ceremony to break the ground," said Grampa. "We only needed to dig a little bit. It will take men younger and stronger than me to build that school-house. Luke, the man with the shovels, is trying to bring together the younger men to build it. He's a good man and has six kids. He needs that school bad."

Then Grampa said, "Meanwhile, you and me need to put our minds together so you can learn your reading and writing here at home. We can't wait for that school to get built."

I was tired. Mama told me to go to bed. I heard the coyotes howl, but they were far away, and I told myself not to be afraid. I felt sleep come over me. But suddenly, there were boys chasing me! I ran away from them—running, running, through the woods—running like the wind. I woke up, my heart pounding. I'd had a scary nightmare.

I was still in bed, and it was dark outside. The moon-light shone on me through my bedroom window, and I sat up and watched the wind blowing the trees. I imagined myself playing up in the treetops. I watched the moon until I felt sleepy. Then I went back to sleep.

The next morning, I woke up wondering why those boys knocked me down. Did I do something wrong? Why did they say, "No Indians allowed?" Was I an Indian, like Mr. Henry? Grampa said I was "white," even though I was very tan. Those boys were just mean and stupid, but I didn't know what to do. Should I tell Grampa? I knew if I did, he would tell Mama and upset her. She might not let me play outside.

As I got dressed, I heard Grampa and Mama talking about the groundbreaking. Since my bedroom was right next to the kitchen, I heard them talking every morning in the kitchen while Mama fixed breakfast and Grampa drank coffee. Usually I didn't pay much attention to their conversations. But this morning, I listened carefully because they were talking about me.

Mama asked Grampa, "How did she do at the groundbreaking?" Grampa answered, "She stuck to me like a shadow."

"Did anyone say anything?" asked Mama.

"The government man said the school would be 'in line with the laws and customs of the State of Alabama.' In other words, it will be white only," said Grampa. "But the government man wasn't looking at Willow. He didn't seem to notice her."

Why were they talking about me? I put on my play clothes and opened my bedroom door. Grampa said, "Morning, Willow."

Mama said, "Morning, Peaches. Here's some porridge for you." After I ate my porridge, I asked if I could go play with Molly. "Yes," said Grampa.

But Molly was doing chores for her mother, so I wandered up to my hideout. I usually felt happy up there. But that day my mind was on what happened to me at the groundbreaking.

Who could I talk to? No one else had seen what happened. It was my secret, and I couldn't tell Mama because I couldn't stand her being sad. If I told Grampa, he'd surely tell Mama, and that would be bad.

What about Molly? She was my best friend. She had told me her secret about liking a cute boy at her church. I kept her secret, but I thought it was silly. Maybe I could tell Molly about the mean boys, but I was sure Molly would tell *her* mother, who would tell *my* mother, and get her all upset.

I remembered Mr. Henry telling his secret about being a Choctaw Indian. That was a serious secret, because if his secret got out, he could get shipped off to Indian Territory. That's why we all promised to keep it secret.

I couldn't think of anyone who would keep my secret and not tell anyone else. I decided I had to keep my secret to myself. They hadn't even started building that schoolhouse yet. I was just going to forget about school and those mean boys.

CHAPTER 6

No Indians in the Public Library

"TELL ME ABOUT THE INDIANS, Grampa," I asked him one rainy Sunday when Mama had gone to church.

"Sit here beside me, Willow, and I will tell you," Grampa said. "Long ago, only the Indian people lived in America. Before Alabama and Mississippi were declared states, Chickasaw Country was huge—stretching across the northern part of Mississippi, as well as half of Tennessee. South of here was Choctaw Country, and east of here was the Cherokees' land, and to the southeast were the Muskoke, or Creek, peoples.

"Did you grow up with Chickasaws as friends?"

"Yes," said Grampa. "My father was one of the first white men to come here, and he became friends with the Chickasaws and asked their permission to settle here. The Chickasaw chief told him where to settle, which was right here where we still live today. This area was part of the Chickasaw hunting grounds, a border area with the Cherokees.

"When I was growing up, my friends were Chickasaw boys. They taught me how to hunt—how to live in the woods. And in the spring, I helped them plant corn and vegetables under the direction of the Chickasaw women. I loved the Chickasaws."

"Then what happened?" I asked.

"Then more white people came here, and many of them didn't like Indians at all. They settled in Indian Country but wanted all the land for themselves. Then Andrew Jackson ran for president, saying that this land was 'only for whites—all the Indians should leave.' Then Jackson became president and got the United States military to force the Chickasaws, Choctaws, Cherokees, Creeks, and Seminoles to leave their sacred homelands and go west to 'Indian Territory.'"

Grampa sighed and stopped talking. His eyes looked sad, like he might cry. He wiped his face with his handkerchief and said, "Some of the Indian people refused to go west. Mr. Burt Henry is one of them. And so is your Auntie Annie. They hid in the hills and mountains. Some, like Mr. Henry, married into dark-skinned families, others into white families. They tried to become white or black, anything to stay on the land they loved."

"Your Auntie Annie," Grampa whispered, "is trying to look like a poor old white woman who is brown from so much farming. It's a secret that she is Chickasaw because, according to the law, Indian people are not allowed to live here anymore."

Grampa looked at me, "Can you keep Auntie Annie's secret? And Mr. Burt Henry's secret?" "Yes, Grampa," I told him, "They are secret Indians. I will keep their secrets."

Some weeks later, Grampa asked me to go with him to Market Town, the big town north of here. "I need to do errands at the public library and the general store. I would like your help," Grampa said.

"Molly loves books. Can she come with us to the library?" I asked.

Grampa sighed, "No, Willow, I'm sorry. They won't let Molly into the library." "Why not?" I asked. "She can read, she's smart!"

"I'll explain why when we ride up there tomorrow."

I couldn't see why Grampa couldn't answer my simple question right then. But I tried to be patient.

The next day, Molly's dad, Mr. Henry, lent Grampa his horse and buggy so we could ride up to Market Town. "It's nice of Mr. Henry to let you take Sugar and the buggy," I said to Grampa as we trotted towards Market Town.

Grampa said he'd always had a horse and buggy--until he lost those buried valuables. "You mean, when the Floozy stole them?" I asked.

"Yes, yes," he said. "I had to sell Pal and my buggy so I could pay our land taxes. Hard times come in many different ways. For me it was that pretty young woman who played me for a fool. And I am still suffering for my mistakes. It hurts to have to walk everywhere."

"We're doing okay," I said, trying to make Grampa feel better.

Grampa paused, "Thank goodness for the Henrys. I traded with them to use their buggy, and they gave me a long list of errands to do for them in Market Town."

"But," I asked, "Why can't Molly come with us to the library?"

Grampa sighed, "You always ask me hard questions." Then he just stared at the road as we trotted along. Finally, Grampa said, "People come in all different shades, some are light- skinned and some are dark-skinned."

"Yes, I know *that*," I answered impatiently, I had heard Grampa say those words more than once. "Underneath those different color skins," I said, mocking his deep voice, "we are all the same."

"Yes," Grampa said, "We all have muscles and bones and brains and hearts and blood. We all want to live, eat, sleep, and have some fun. All of us—regardless of our skin color."

Grampa paused for what seemed like forever as Sugar kept trotting towards Market Town. Suddenly, he started talking again, "But too many light-skinned people think they are superior to dark-skinned people. They think that public schools and public libraries should *only* be for white people."

"That's not fair!" I said. "Molly is so smart ..."

"You're right. It's *not* fair. Molly is very smart and she wants to learn," said Grampa. "But 'separation of the races' is the law here in Alabama and most everywhere in this country."

"Are we tan, Grampa?" I asked, holding my arm next to Grampa's. "Yes," said Grampa. "But we are considered 'white.'"

Grampa stopped talking, and Sugar kept trotting towards Market Town. Then Grampa said, "At the groundbreaking, do you remember when that government man said, 'All will be according to the laws of the State of Alabama'? He meant that the school they are building is for white children only."

"How can they do that?" I cried.

But Grampa didn't answer me. We had gotten to Market Town, and he was pointing out the big general store, the fancy hotel, and the Market Town Public Library.

"What kind of books would you like to borrow from the library?" Grampa asked me.

It only took me only a second to decide: "I would like to get books about the Chickasaws and Choctaws. I want to learn about Mr. Henry's people and Auntie Annie's people."

Then Grampa pulled into a lot where there were some horses and buggies and guided Sugar to a shade tree. "We're going to let Sugar rest here," he told me, "while we do our errands."

First, we went to the library. Grampa was right. There were only light-skinned people in there, except for one dark-skinned man in work clothes who was fixing a cracked table. I couldn't see any reason Molly should be kept out of this library.

Grampa showed me the library's card catalog, with little drawers that held an index card for each and every book in the library. There were lots of drawers. Grampa looked into the drawer labeled C. It had cards in it for every book on subjects beginning with the letter C. But there were no cards for books about Chickasaws or Choctaws. "We will ask the librarian to help us," said Grampa, and we went up to the library desk, and Grampa asked the librarian about books on the Chickasaws and Choctaws.

"You mean about Indians?" the librarian asked us. And Grampa nodded yes.

"Hmmm, let me see," said the librarian. But she couldn't find anything about Chickasaws or Choctaws.

"What about history of Alabama or Mississippi a hundred years ago, before they became states?" Grampa asked. That didn't work either. There were books on Alabama history, but they all started when Alabama became a state in 1819.

"The Chickasaws and Choctaws lived here for thousands of years before Alabama became a state," Grampa told the librarian.

"Sorry," said the librarian, "no books here on Chickasaws or Choctaws."

Grampa asked me if I wanted to look at picture books and pointed to the bookshelves with children's books. I looked at those books, and some of them smelled funny. I handed one to Grampa, and he said, "Yup, it smells moldy."

I didn't like the library.

Grampa had work he needed to do in the library, so I went outside and patted Sugar. I was glad when Grampa finally came out of there. He handed me a book called *Picture Book of ABCs*, and it smelled okay. He also borrowed a library book for Molly called *Birmingham: City of Progress*.

Then we took our baskets into the Market Town General Store, and looked for all kinds of things on both Grampa's list and Miz Mildred's list. I saw a girl about my size shopping with her mother. They were dark-skinned. I smiled at her, and she shyly smiled back at me. When we finished with the long lists, we stood in line to pay. I saw the girl and her mother standing off to the side. When we were next in line to pay, I whispered to Grampa, "That girl and her mother have been waiting longer than us." Grampa acted like he hadn't heard me and proceeded to the cash register. I looked at the girl, and she looked at the floor.

When we left the general store with all our stuff, I asked Grampa, "Why did you pay before the brown-skinned mother and little girl?"

"Because that is the custom here in the South," he said gruffly as we walked to the Henrys' horse and buggy.

"That's not fair." I said.

"You're right. I don't like it. But it's the way it is." He paused and then added, "That's why I do the Henrys' shopping for them, so they don't have to wait off to the side until all the white people have paid."

After we packed all the things into the buggy, Grampa said that he needed to go to the government tax office. I told him I would rather stay with Sugar. I stretched out on the seat of the buggy. I looked at the pictures in the ABC book. It was comfortable there under the cool of the tree, and I felt sleepy. The next thing I knew, Grampa woke me up.

"Last stop is Berta's," announced Grampa. "Another stop?" I complained.

"I saved the best for last," said Grampa. "Miz Berta has a beautiful herb garden. You will love it."

We went to Miz Berta's, and Grampa was right. I could've stayed all day in that garden. Miz Berta was real nice. She had dark brown skin and very curly dark hair. Grampa bought some of her dried herbs for his achy feet and ankles.

On the way home, Grampa said, "Miz Berta's been healing people with herbs for a long time. She's a midwife—for decades she's helped birthing almost every baby born 'round here."

Grampa stopped talking and we traveled on in silence. Then he began talking again, "Years ago, after the Indians had to go west, I helped heal the men folks, using what I had been taught by a Chickasaw medicine man. At the same time, Miz Berta was healing the women and children.

"We both used some of the old-time methods passed down by the Chickasaws. But so much wisdom of the Chickasaws was lost when they had to go west. I gave up trying to be a healer. But Miz Berta, she kept on growing herbs, healing folks, and birthing babies."

In late November it suddenly got cold. Jack Frost came and ice sparkled on the grass. I didn't like the cold. It meant I couldn't run around in my bare feet. It meant I had to wear shoes and a long heavy skirt, a sweater, and sometimes a heavy jacket.

The frost stayed for two days, and the cold killed the corn and the squash—the crops we had planned to pick in our late harvest. "Grampa—all our crops are dead!" I cried at dinner that night.

"The cold is good for us," said Mama. But I didn't believe Mama. I thought it was just because she liked to be inside.

"Mama Rose is right," said Grampa. "Plants worked hard all through the warm season, and now they need to rest in the winter. We had a good harvest this year and collected plenty of seeds that we will plant next spring."

"But Grampa, why did all that squash and corn we left for the late harvest have to die?" I tried to hold back my tears.

"Well, Jack Frost caught us by surprise. He's a trickster."

"Is there a way we can tell when he's coming?"

Grampa sat there, shaking his head sadly. "The Chickasaws used to be able to read the signs and know when to pull the last harvest. But I never learned those signs from them, and then my Chickasaw friends were forced to leave and take all that wisdom with them."

CHAPTER 7
Mama's Story

A S THE WINTER COLD DESCENDED on us, we looked forward to Christmas. My brother Thomas was coming home, and Mama and I cleaned the whole house. Grampa and I cut down a small pine tree to decorate for the living room. We made popcorn and sewed them into garlands to hang on it. Mama got out her old decorations, and they looked real pretty on our Christmas tree.

Mama couldn't wait to see Thomas. All week, Mama had been baking pies and breads. She was happy, and that made me happy. I began to understand why she liked cooking. "It's wonderful to feed the people you love," she told me.

On Christmas Eve, Grampa borrowed Mr. Henry's horse and buggy to pick up Thomas in Market Town, where the public coach from Birmingham would bring him. Mama got her pretty tablecloth and her fine china out of the sideboard. We washed the china and set the table for Christmas Eve dinner.

"Willow, why don't you go and invite Molly, Miz Mildred, and Mr. Henry to come over tomorrow night for Christmas dessert," she said.

"That will be fun!" I said. And I went next door to invite the Henrys. They said they would love to come and see Thomas again.

Mama was in a good mood. She talked about the Christmas when she was pregnant with little Thomas and her husband was still alive. Mama missed her son, and I got tired of hearing her talk about Thomas, so I asked her to tell me a story about *me*—when I was little. She told me how sad she was after her husband's and her brother's deaths.

"That war was a terrible thing," Mama said. "But then *you* came along and made me very happy." That made me feel loved, and I told her how much I loved her. It felt good to see my mama happy.

But that beautiful day suddenly ended. Grampa came home all by himself. Thomas was not with him. The coachman had given Grampa a letter from Aunt Frida, which said:

Dear Jack and Rose,

Thomas is not coming to your house for Christmas. He refused to come out of his bedroom this morning to catch the public coach to Market Town.

Thomas has been having difficulty in school this fall. Last week he was expelled from his boarding school because of his temper tantrums. We pray for better times in the new year.

Yours truly,
Mrs. Andrew Fields

Mama started to cry. She went to her bedroom and closed the door. I went next door to tell the Henrys that

Thomas was not coming. The next day was Christmas, a sad one for us. In the morning, I was surprised to see Grampa packing his suitcase. He told me he was going to Birmingham to see Thomas. Grampa told me to take care of Mama. If she stayed in her bedroom, I should fix her meals and bring them to her. Grampa also told me that the Henrys invited me over to celebrate Christmas with them. "Take Mama's sweet potato pie over there to share with them," he said.

Mama stayed in her bedroom, and I took breakfast to her. She was still sleeping, so I left the plate on her bedside table. Then I went next door to the Henrys with the pie.

At the Henrys, everybody was having a Merry Christmas. Miz Mildred's sister and her three kids were visiting, and there was lots of commotion. Miz Mildred gave me a big hug and told me I was part of their family. But I felt gloomy. I noticed Mr. Henry sitting by himself, tending the fireplace. I went and sat next to him. I asked him, "Do you ever miss your Choctaw family?"

"Yes, I do." Mr. Henry said, smiling, "I was very young, but I remember our winter feasts when every family brought food, and we made a big fire. We danced and sang around the fire to stay warm. Afterwards, we crowded into somebody's house to tell stories. I don't remember the stories. I was little. I must've fallen asleep."

After dinner and pie at the Henrys' I came back home. The house was dark and Mama was still in her bedroom. The next day, Mama got up and we cooked together. A few days later, Mama got a letter from Grampa. He said he was going to stay with Thomas in

Birmingham to try to get him back in his school. Our house felt empty. I helped Mama in the kitchen. She told me she was a failure as a mother. I told her she was a wonderful mother.

The next morning Mama gave me my presents, which had been lying in their wrapping paper under the tree since Christmas. There were two books. One was *My First Reader*, and the other was *Grimm's Fairy Tales*. I looked at them, wishing I was looking at a book about the Indians who used to live here.

We made biscuits and ate them with mint jelly. We had good talks. But a few days later, Mama got sad again. When I said something to her, she looked right through me as if I wasn't there.

She cooked in the morning, and then sat at the kitchen table all day, lost in thought.

I went outside and took care of the animals and brought in wood. I wandered around outside, but it was cold. Then I went back and sat in the kitchen because it was the only warm spot.

Mama was still staring into the distance, no longer talking. I was restless and worried. What was wrong with Mama?

Then we got a letter in our mailbox addressed to both Mama and me. Mama read it to me:

Dear Rose and Willow,

I have been staying in Birmingham with Thomas and his Uncle Andrew and Aunt Frida. Thomas and I have spent a lot of time together, and I think we are becoming good friends again.

I've been corresponding with his school, and in two weeks we are going there to see if they will readmit Thomas based on improved behavior.

I will be in Birmingham for at least three more weeks. Please stay warm and healthy.

Love from, Jack

I didn't want Grampa to stay away three more long weeks! I missed him. The house felt empty with just me and Mama.

But Mama perked up. "Thomas is doing better. I am so relieved." Grampa's letter made Mama feel happy, and the next morning I woke up to the smell of eggs and grits. Mama sat down to eat with me.

"Willow," she said, "it looks like we will be spending more time with just the two of us, since Grampa's gonna be away for a while longer."

She paused. "I know you like to be outside, and I know you don't like to cook. But it is wintertime, and I would like you to spend more time with me in the kitchen—so I don't get so lonely. And I will try to answer your questions."

Mama and I made a deal. She got my help in the kitchen, and I got to ask her questions that she promised to answer.

"Mama, can you tell me about when you were a girl?"

Mama said, "I was born in 1838. I grew up hearing the terrible things done to the Indians—driving them out of their homeland. Up here in the hills, many of the early white settlers had been marrying Indians for generations. I grew up right after the Indian Removal, and there still were Chickasaws, Choctaws, and Cherokees around here.

48

They were Indians who refused to leave and hid in the hills. Many people around here had Indians in their families. They were trying to blend in with the white folks so they wouldn't get sent out west.

"When I was coming of age," Mama continued, "slavery became the big issue. Up here in the northern hills, there weren't many slaves because the land was hilly and rocky, and people barely grew enough to feed their families. South of here, on the flat fertile land, were the big plantations.

"But my grandfather owned a family of Negroes, who came with him when he moved here from Georgia. When he died shortly before the Civil War, my father—who is your Grampa—inherited that colored family. But your Grampa hated slavery. I remember your Grampa saying, 'These are human beings—I refuse to own people!'

"Your Grampa freed that family of nine people. The young folks in that family went north to seek freedom. The elderly parents stayed here, along with Mildred, who was their youngest child. Mildred and I grew up together. We've known each other our whole lives."

Mama explained that when Grampa freed Mildred's family, some white people turned against him. They disagreed with Grampa that 'all people are created equal.' Very few colored people lived around here. Even though most white people up here did not own slaves, they still thought they were better than Negroes.

"When the South left the Union and went to war, Grampa became a Unionist," Mama continued,"—he was against the Confederacy, against going to war so the plantation owners could keep their slaves. A good number of men in northern Alabama were Unionists.

"That's enough story for today," said Mama, wiping her brow. "I need to cook dinner, and you have chores to do." Then she added, "Tomorrow—God willing—I'll tell you more."

I did my chores, thinking about Mama saying, "God willing," about something she planned to do the next day. It was like she expected something bad to happen to stop her plans. That must be a hard way to live, I thought. For me, I expected the sun to come up every morning. I expected to eat breakfast and feed the animals, do chores, and play with Molly.

I got the animals into the barn while Mama fixed supper. That night Mama was in a good mood. After dinner, Mama read me some stories from my new book, *Grimm's Fairy Tales*. I liked the story "Cinderella," about a poor girl who goes to the ball and wins the heart of the prince. Then Mama read "Rapunzel," a story I did not like. Why would Rapunzel want some boy climbing up her hair?

That night, I woke with a start. What was that noise? It sounded like the teakettle, boiling on the stove. I jumped out of bed, ran into the kitchen, and took the whistling kettle off the stove.

Mama was sitting at the table, her head resting on her arms, fast asleep. "Mama, are you okay?" I asked.

"Oh dear," she mumbled as she woke up. "Trouble sleeping." Then she shuffled back to her bedroom.

CHAPTER 8

Mama's Very Sad Story

THE NEXT MORNING, MAMA SLEPT late. I fixed breakfast for her, and planned to take it to her bedroom. But she came into the kitchen, sat down, and ate her breakfast. She said nothing for a long time. She looked tired, haggard—and closed her eyes. I thought she had gone back to sleep, sitting at the table. But then she shook herself, opened her eyes, and looked at me. "Today I will tell you my sad story," she said.

"You don't have to tell it," I whispered to her.

"I *need* to tell it today, because today is February 28," she said. "Thirteen years ago was when my Thomas was killed."

After chores, we sat down in the kitchen, and Mama poured us tea. Then she started her story about growing up with her mother and father, sister and brother, right here in this house. Her daddy was the county judge, and our house was his courthouse as well as where his family lived. They had a farm, which we still have, and raised the food they ate.

"I thought I would be an old maid," Mama said, "because I turned twenty and never had a boyfriend. It seemed like my place was in this house, in the kitchen, cooking for my daddy.

"But one day, this handsome young man came home with my daddy. He was my daddy's new assistant. His name was Thomas, and I fell in love at first sight. He courted me like a perfect gentleman. On our first date he told me that he, like my daddy, was against slavery. Thomas was from a wealthy Birmingham family who owned lots of slaves. But he vowed to *never* own people—and broke with his family over slavery. He respected my daddy and our family, and wanted to learn from us.

"Thomas and I got married in June 1860, right here in this yard. It was a big old country-style wedding. In those days we were better off than we are now, so we had lots of guests, lots of food and drink. It was a beautiful wedding. That fall I realized I was pregnant with our child. Thomas was thrilled. There was lots of talk of war at that time. But to me, the world seemed perfect.

"In November 1860, Abraham Lincoln was elected President of the United States. Southern white men talked about breaking away from the United States and creating the Confederate States of America. Daddy and Thomas were Unionists, which meant they wanted to stay part of the United States.

"Many people up here in this part of Alabama were Unionists because they were poor farmers who did not want to die so the rich could keep slaves. The State of Alabama took a vote on secession that December. Of course, only the white men could vote. Up here in the northern hills of Alabama, most voted for continuing to be part of the United States. But in the rest of Alabama, the majority voted to pull out of the Union. In January 1861, the State of Alabama seceded from the US and joined the Confederacy. Then the Civil War began.

"I helped my mother with the cooking and gardening. We knew lots of people who opposed the war. But we also had enemies, and one of those enemies killed my husband. We never found out who did it."

Mama took out her hankie, wiped her eyes, and blew her nose. She took a deep sigh and rested her head on her folded arms. She just seemed to disappear inside herself. I fixed her some more tea, but it didn't do any good.

Then she whispered, "Thirteen years ago today, in the morning, they killed my Thomas. If only Thomas had stayed home with me that day..."

"Poor Mama!" I cried. I didn't know what to do. Should I hug her? Kiss her?

"It's okay, Willow," she said, wiping her eyes. "You are with me, and that's what I need. I will tell you the story of that day if you want to listen."

"I want to hear your story, Mama."

"It was a cold winter morning," Mama said. "While I fixed breakfast, my husband and my father talked about Thomas riding up to Market Town that day. Thomas kissed me goodbye, got his horse out of the barn and rode off to Market Town, just like any other day.

"Then I heard a loud bang. I ran out the front door and I saw Thomas' horse gallop by—with an empty saddle! I screamed, and my daddy grabbed his gun. We ran down the road looking for Thomas. We found him lying on the ground—dead—shot through the heart."

Mama whispered, "Every year on this day, I go to the spot where Thomas fell. "Will you come with me today?"

"Yes, Mama, I will."

It was a cold and windy day, and we bundled up in our coats and hats. We walked through the small family cemetery next to the house. Mama touched her husband's tombstone. "I see this grave every day, but on this day I have to go to where he lost his life." Mama headed up the road towards Market Town, and I started to feel scared. We walked a ways. Then Mama turned and headed into the brush on the left side of the road where there used to be an Indian path.

As she climbed through the bushes, Mama whispered to me, "I always feel spirits here. But they are kind spirits—they won't hurt you." She stopped at the spot where Thomas had fallen, which Grampa had marked with a large flat rock. Opening her arms wide, Mama looked up at the sky and then down at the dirt. Then she lay down and put her arms around that rock and cried. I stood there looking up at the wind as it rushed through the branches. I felt my heart pounding. The earth was beating like a huge heart. Must be the spirits, I thought. Up above, angry clouds rushed by. I imagined myself up there, howling in the wind, howling with my mama's pain.

Slowly I calmed down. But poor Mama—she lay on that rock for a long time. Finally, she got up and wiped her eyes with her kerchief. Silently, we walked back home.

"Ever since the day Thomas was killed, I've come back to this spot every February 28. I've never taken anyone with me until today, when you came with me. Thank you, Willow, for coming with me."

After we came back into the house, we stood in the kitchen, and Mama spoke again. "The day they killed my husband, I forgot I had a baby growing in me. But that night I felt it kicking inside me like a little frog. That spring, I bore this little baby boy and I named him Thomas, after his father. I loved that baby. The Civil War went on and on, but I didn't think about the war. I just took care of my baby and cooked for my father."

Then Mama went into her bedroom and shut the door. I heard her weeping in there. After a while there was silence. She must have fallen asleep. I went into the kitchen and found some cornbread and molasses to eat for supper.

The next morning, Mama started talking again. I didn't even have to ask her a question.

"It does me good to tell you about my beloved husband." she said. "All these memories have been bottled up inside me, waiting to come out.

"During the war, my daddy was so strong in opposing the Confederacy," she continued. "Some time in the middle of the war, the Confederate Army told my father that they were coming to his courthouse to recruit for their army. Daddy told his friends, who were Unionists, about the Confederates' plan, and they told their friends.

"The Confederates were coming to this house because it was the county courthouse. They came determined to recruit for their Confederate Army. But they found over one hundred armed Unionists in the courthouse yard and the Union flag flying from the flag pole! Words were exchanged, and after a while those Confederates left. Not a shot was fired.

"I was inside the court house—this house—sitting right there on the floor under that front window. I held my baby and prayed. I feared we would all die that day. But those Confederates saw all those armed Unionists—and they left. When all was said and done that day, I was proud of my daddy and his friends for standing up to that army.

"But the war went on and on. Things got worse and worse for us common folks. The Confederates forced all the young men into the Confederate Army. They got my brother, Robert. He was only seventeen, and he was in the army for barely a month when he died of fever. We buried my brother next to my husband.

"Robert's death hit your Grampa hard. He took down the Union flag and just let the flagpole stand there with no flag. The war went on and on, and people starved. We were lucky. We didn't starve because we farmed, and I learned how to stretch the food to feed lots of people.

"Finally, the war ended. What a relief. But my daddy was no longer popular with the Alabama government. They moved the courthouse to Market Town. They elected a different county judge. It was just me, Daddy, Mama, and little Thomas living here in this house.

"But then my dead husband's family wanted my boy to come live with them in Birmingham. They said they would pay for little Thomas to go to boarding school.

"We said, 'No, we will educate him here.' My daddy was determined to educate little Thomas, and also little Molly Henry, who was the same age and lived next door. My daddy—your Grampa—had two little pupils, and he put a lot of effort into educating them.

"When little Thomas turned eight, his uncle tried again to get him to go to school down in Birmingham. People around here were still divided. Our village still didn't have a schoolhouse, and no prospect of building one. My husband's parents—pro-Confederate, high-falutin' rich folks—insisted that Thomas should go to live with them and go to boarding school with their sons.

"I said no, but Thomas said he liked his cousins and wanted to live with them and go to school. And that's how I lost my second Thomas."

"Oh Mama," I said, "that is a sad, sad story."

The next morning, I woke up with a question: Who was *my* daddy? Mama's husband could not be my daddy, because he died during the War, many years before I was born. Who was my daddy?

The next day, I helped Mama cook cornbread to sell at the Pine Hill Grocery Store. As we walked to the store, I asked a hard question. "Mama, who is my daddy? Your husband got killed in 1861 and I was born years later. Your Thomas is not my daddy, right?"

"You're right," said Mama. "And you are old enough to know the truth. But I can't tell you while we are out here in the public. Wait till we're back in the house."

We got to the grocery store, and Mama gave Mr. Johnson the cornbread she had cooked. Then Mama bought some flour to make biscuits and she also bought me a candy cane, which I started sucking right away. We got home, made supper, and cleaned up the kitchen. I wanted to remind Mama of her promise to tell me, but I held myself back.

When we sat down with our tea, Mama answered my question. "Willow, darling," she said, "the truth is *I don't know who your father is*. I am your mother now, but I was not always your mother."

"You weren't?"

"No, I did not bring you into this world. I don't know anything about the mother who gave you birth. But I do know who you could ask."

"Who?"

"Your Auntie who visits in the fall. She is the one who brought you to us. I know her name is Annie and that she is Chickasaw. I know her people went through very hard times during and after the war. But other than that, I don't know anything about her. She seems like a real good person. She was looking for someone to take care of you, and she wanted to find folks who saw people as people, regardless of their skin color. And she found us."

Mama sipped her tea, "Every fall, your Auntie walks for two days to come see you. I told you to call her Auntie because people often call a woman 'Auntie' when they are fond of her, even if they are not related. But I believe Auntie is related to you."

Wow. That gave me a lot to think about. That night when the coyotes howled, I looked out my window at the faint silver moon. I couldn't wait to see Auntie in the fall. I had so many questions to ask her.

No wonder Mama and I were so different— in color, in what we liked to do. But I knew Mama loved me, and I loved her. The next morning, I asked Mama, "Tell me about when you first saw me."

Mama answered me right away. "It was about a year after my son Thomas left to go to boarding school in Birmingham," she said. "I missed my little son so much. Then the Chickasaw chief of Auntie's village came by and talked to Grampa. He knew that this family had been good friends of the Chickasaws for generations. The chief talked to Grampa about this little child who needed a home.

"That night, my father told me about the chief's visit. I said, 'I would like to meet this little child.' Then I met you, and I fell in love with you at first sight!"

Mama reached out and hugged me and kissed me, but I had another question: "Mama, do you love me as much as you love little Thomas?"

"You can't stop asking these hard questions!" Mama laughed. "Yes, I *do* love you as much as I love little Thomas. In fact, can you keep another secret?"

"Yes," I said. "I'm good at keeping secrets."

"I love you *more*," said Mama. "Because you are still here with me. And because I *know* you love me."

I felt close to Mama after she told me all those stories. She wasn't my birth mother. I knew nothing about my birth mother. But I knew I loved my Mama Rose.

CHAPTER 9

Sawyers

A S TIME WENT ON, GRAMPA'S feet hurt him more
and more. When I turned eight, Grampa needed
a cane in order to walk. Mama heated up water
on the stove every night so Grampa could soak his feet in
warm water with salts. Grampa's feet slowed down our
spring planting because he couldn't do much. Molly and
I had to do more, and the planting took longer than usual.

The day we finished planting, Molly and I watched
Grampa as he limped slowly out to the middle of our
cornfield. He held what looked like a piece of burned
wood in his hand. We watched as Grampa held up the
burned wood and looked towards the sky, first to the
south, then west, north, and east. Grampa saw us watching him. "It's lightning wood," he explained to us, "—
special medicine for the corn crop." And then he buried
that lightning wood right in the middle of our cornfield.

A few weeks later, the weather got hot and then the
rains came. Molly and I had to do lots of hoeing to keep
those weeds from smothering our crops. The corn in our
field grew especially fast with the help from Grampa's
lightening wood.

In July, we went to the farm animal fair in Market
Town. Grampa, Mr. and Mrs. Henry, Molly, and I all

crammed into Mr. Henry's wagon and set off to look at the animals. Our families had been saving money from last year's bumper crop, and we came home with a pregnant cow, two baby pigs, a little donkey, and a dozen baby chicks. Mama and Miz Mildred were very happy about the new cow, because it meant more milk for making pies and cakes to sell at the grocery store. Grampa and Mr. Henry taught me and Molly how to take care of the new animals.

A few weeks later, Mr. Henry came home from Birmingham in a new buggy pulled by a new horse. Mr. Henry named his new horse Partner, and he told us he was going to take on work as a hack driver in Market Town. A hack driver drives people around who don't have a horse and buggy. Mr. Henry had driven a hack in Birmingham, and his former boss there had sold him the horse and buggy on credit, which meant he had to make monthly payments. Mr. Henry said driving a hack was a good way to make some money. "Market Town is growing," he told us. "People come there by public coach and need hack drivers to taxi them around town."

Grampa talked about making some money by tutoring children in Pine Hill, but he could no longer walk that far. So he traded with Mr. Henry to get Sugar, Mr. Henry's horse, and his old buggy. We finally had a horse and buggy again. Grampa started going into Pine Hill every week to tutor kids who lived there.

The dog days of summer arrived. It was so hot and dry that all I could think about was swimming in the pond. But even the pond water got too warm for me. At dawn one morning two big men came over. They were George and Rick Sawyer, and they liked to dig holes and take down trees. Before I woke up that morning, they started shoveling a big hole in the woods between our house and the Henrys' house. When I went to do my morning business, the Sawyers were digging away, not far from where I sat in our outhouse. I realized they were digging us a new latrine.

"Good," I thought. "This old latrine is falling apart. Grampa said it smells like the Devil's outhouse."

The Sawyer brothers tore down the old outhouse and filled in the hole with sticks and leaves and dirt. Then they built a new outhouse over the new hole. It had two rooms, each with its own door. One faced the Henrys' house, and the other faced our house.

That night Grampa asked me, "Should we ask the Sawyers to help us get ready for the cold winter weather now?"

I said, "No, it's too hot. Chopping wood is hard work, and it is months before we'll need it."

"That's true," said Grampa, "but we can't chop down trees or cut them up to the right size for our woodstoves by ourselves. We need help. The Sawyers are good at doing that work. Years ago, when you were knee high to a grasshopper, they came and cut down four big, dead trees. By now we've used up almost all that firewood."

"But it's a long time before Jack Frost comes."

"The Sawyers are coming back here tomorrow," Grampa told me. "They can give us three days' work now, whereas in the fall they get real busy working for other people."

Early the next morning, George and Rick Sawyer arrived in their horse and wagon. They had a two-person crosscut saw which they used to take down big trees.

Grampa showed them the dead oak and elm trees he wanted taken down.

The Sawyer brothers were very serious. But they brought fun with them--their kids! Their three girls were all around my age. Their names were Sue Ann, who was age eight like me, Clara Louise—age seven, and Peggy Lynn, who was six. With me and Molly, there were five of us girls, and we had a good time.

While Grampa and Mr. Henry worked with the two men, us kids had the job of collecting kindling. Wood was how Mama and Miz Mildred cooked all year—and how we kept warm in winter. We needed lots of logs to be sawed to a certain size. We also needed lots of sticks and smaller pieces of wood, called kindling. Collecting sticks is an important job because, without kindling, you can't get the logs to catch fire. "There's nothing worse than running out of kindling when it cold outside," Grampa taught me. "All the logs in the world are useless if you don't have dry sticks to get the fire started."

After the Sawyers arrived, Mr. Henry gave a bushel basket to each of us kids. "You five girls need to fill these baskets up with kindling and dump it into the big bins in the woodshed. I want to see those two kindling bins filled to the top. We need you to help us 'keep the home fires burning.'"

Basket in hand, we girls headed for the woods. We filled up those baskets and broke up the sticks to be the right size for the woodstoves. Then we dumped the baskets into the big kindling bins in the woodshed. The woodshed stood between our two houses. One side faced Molly's house and the other side faced my house.

Three times that first day, we had to stop because the grownups called us to come over to them. The Sawyers were about to fell a big tree, and they didn't want that tree to fall on any of us. We stood with Grampa and Mr. Henry, and it was exciting to watch. The brothers stood under that tree for a long time, figuring out where they wanted the tree to fall and how to make it fall exactly where they wanted. They didn't start sawing until we girls stood holding hands with each other and Grampa and Mr. Henry. We all carefully watched the Sawyers take their big crosscut saw and begin sawing. They sawed a notch on the tree, looked around, then sawed it deeper. After what felt like a long time, the tree started to fall. We all yelled, "Timber!" And the tree crashed down, sending leaves and branches and dirt into the air. And we yelled, "Hurray!"

The Sawyers cut down the dead trees, all of them very tall with lots of dry wood, good for fires. And when they finished felling the trees, they called it a day. Everyone was hot and tired. We needed to get lots of rest so we could do more work the next day.

When the Sawyers came back the next morning, they measured the tree trunks with a string, making chalk marks every 18 inches. With their big crosscut saw, they cut up the tree into logs that were 18 inches long, the proper lengths for the Henrys' and our wood stoves. These logs would keep our houses warm on cold winter nights. But winter seemed a long way off. The Sawyer brothers were sweating like crazy, and they jumped in the pond before lunch. After lunch and a rest, they stood the big logs up on their ends.

Meanwhile, us kids filled up the kindling bins to the very top. There was still lots of kindling wood on those felled trees, and we made brush piles of the small branches so that we could use them as kindling when bins became empty.

Thank goodness, on the third day it was cooler. The grownups used axes to split the logs for our woodstoves. They needed us to stay away from where they were swinging their axes. So we went out to the meadow beyond the cornfields and played. We had races. My favorite race was the long race all the way around the whole meadow. I won that race! It felt so good to run.

That day I noticed lots of things about our friends. Sue Ann was the biggest. She was my age but almost as big as Molly, and she had straight black hair and brown eyes— and she was very tan.

Clara Louise looked like Sue Ann, but her eyes were green. Peggy Lynn looked different, with pale skin, blond curly hair, and blue eyes.

After we said goodbye to the Sawyers, Grampa told me his feet were sore, so I set up the soaking tub for him. He sat on the big rocking chair and soaked his feet in warm water. I figured that was a good time to ask him a question.

I asked Grampa about the Sawyer brothers and their young'uns with the different colored eyes, hair, and skin. Grampa explained, "Those girls are cousins, their fathers are brothers. The older brother married an Indian woman, so Sue Ann and Clara Louise look like a mixture of their mother and father. The younger brother married a woman with blond hair and blue eyes, so Peggy Lynn has lighter coloring.

"Sue Ann's and Clara Louise's mother is an Indian?" I asked. "Yes," said Grampa. "She's Chickasaw."

"Are Indians *colored*?"

"The State of Alabama says they are. I think they are people, just like us."

CHAPTER 10

Schoolhouse Built

ONE DAY IN MID-AUGUST, not long after the Sawyers were finished at our house, Grampa came back from the Pine Hill village with "big news." At dinner he announced, "The new schoolhouse is built! School is opening in September!"

"Oh no!" I felt like I had been punched in the stomach. "I don't want to go to that school!" "Why not?" asked Grampa.

"It's just for white kids, colored are not allowed!"

"Stop shouting." said Mama.

"It's true that the school is white-only," said Grampa calmly. "But there aren't any Negro children here, except for Molly, and she's been home-schooled."

I *almost* said, "Look at my brown skin—I'm colored too!" But I held my tongue. After finishing what was on my plate, I ran outside. I wanted to talk to Molly, but she was in Birmingham. So I went to my hideout and sat up on the ledge for a long time. The breeze picked up, and I talked to it. "I won't go to that school," I told the wind. "I'll hide in the woods."

That night, those mean boys chased me in my dreams, but this time I ran faster and faster, until I flew away. Then I laughed at them because they couldn't catch me.

Molly came home from Birmingham and told me about the fun she had. I told her I didn't want to go to Pine Hill School. Molly said, "I wouldn't want to go to that school either." But I didn't tell her about those boys who knocked me over. I wanted to forget those boys.

Molly and I hoed the cornfields together, and we helped our mothers weed the vegetable gardens. One day at supper, Grampa talked about the school again. "School prepares you for your future," he said.

"I won't go!" I yelled loud, stomping my foot. "I won't go!" I said over and over. "I won't go!" Then Mama punished me for yelling and sent me to bed without supper.

That night, the nightmares came again—worse than before. I was on my way to school and those three mean boys chased me. I was running, running, running away from them—and then I tripped! Those rowdy boys caught me....

I woke up screaming.

Mama came running into my room. I sobbed, out of breath. She sat on the bed and hugged me. I couldn't stop crying.

Then I blurted out to Mama what happened at the groundbreaking last summer: "Those boys bumped into me while Grampa was shoveling—knocked me to the ground! They said I didn't belong in a white school. They said *Indians not allowed—colored not allowed— You're dead!*"

"Oh dear!" cried Mama. "You've been holding this inside for a year? Why didn't you tell us?"

"I don't know," I sobbed. "I didn't want to think about it. It made me feel bad. Then I forgot about it."

"We need to tell Grampa," said Mama calmly.

"No—no!" I cried. "Mama, you can't tell Grampa! It's *my secret!* You are the only one I've told." Then we heard Grampa's limping footsteps, and he appeared at my door, cane in hand.

"What is going on?" he asked.

"Willow says that at the school groundbreaking..." Mama started. "No Mama! *You can't tell him!*" I yelled.

"Willow, we *have* to tell him," Mama said firmly.

Then Grampa raised his voice. "Willow, I am your grandfather. You need to tell me." He stood there leaning on his cane, looking like he was in pain.

Mama stood up and looked at Grampa, "Time for tea at the kitchen table," she said in her voice that meant business. "We need to sit down and talk this through. Now!"

We walked out of my bedroom into the kitchen. Grampa sat down and put his leg up on the chair next to him. I could see that his ankle was swollen, so I got him a pillow and put it under his foot on the chair. Mama made tea and served it with some leftover muffins. I was hungry, and the muffins tasted good.

Mama started to talk. "Willow," she said softly. "Your secret is too big to keep hidden in a small family like ours. You need to spill the beans. It's better to tell someone you trust, rather than keep it bottled up inside."

Grampa said, "I love you Willow. Please tell me what's bothering you. Maybe I can help."

I told Grampa, "Last year at the groundbreaking, you were shoveling with your back to me. Those mean boys ran by me. They knocked me over, saying—*this is a white-only school, Indians not allowed*, and *You're dead!*"

There was silence in the kitchen. "Why, that's terrible! For goodness sake, why didn't you tell me?" asked Grampa.

"I don't know," I whimpered, feeling stupid for keeping it secret. I cried and cried some more. Mama took a pie out of the cupboard, a blackberry pie she had made that day. We ate the whole thing. Then we all went to our beds and fell asleep.

The next day, Grampa told me, "Willow, we are *not* going to let anyone hurt you. I've been thinking about your safety at this school. All of us—you, me, and your mama—are going to the new school together on the first day. I will be in that classroom to be sure those boys do not touch you. I like the new teacher, and I will ask to be her volunteer assistant so I can be in that classroom every day."

I said, "Grampa, you can't turn your back on me, not even for a second!"

And Grampa agreed. He was determined I was going to school. And he promised to not let anyone hurt me.

In September, the Pine Hill Public School opened. Grampa and Mama waited for me in the buggy.

"Hurry up, Willow," called Grampa. "We can't be late for your first day of school."

I was looking at the sunflowers in Mama's garden. I had my new dress on—the green and yellow one that Mama had sewed for me—with the same colors as the sunflowers. Mama had braided my hair in two plaits that hung down my back. "You look so nice," Mama said. But I didn't feel nice. My stomach hurt and my head ached.

Sugar trotted along pulling the buggy, and soon we got to the new schoolhouse. It looked nice with its brand-new coat of white paint, sitting right between the church and the grocery store. Someone had even planted flowers next to the schoolhouse steps.

We got to school right on time, just as everyone was going inside. There were lots of children, and some looked familiar. But I didn't know any of their names. The teacher clapped her hands, saying, "Good morning, children. I am Miss Leslie, your teacher at the new Pine Hill Public School."

Then she pointed to Grampa, who was standing next to the rowdy boys, and said, "This is my assistant teacher, Mr. Farrell." Everyone turned and looked at Grampa.

"Mothers, please leave the classroom," Miss Leslie continued. "Tell your children you will see them after class is dismissed."

I hugged Mama hard. She told me she was going next door to the Pine Hill Grocery Store and would be right outside when school was over. I looked around. Kids were talking to their friends. Everyone seemed to have a friend, except me.

"Line up in size order," Miss Leslie said, "Cindy, here, is the smallest, and the biggest is Bill, standing in the back of the room near Mr. Farrell. I am going to assign a seat to each of you."

We lined up and I counted twenty-two children. I was the ninth smallest, even though I was eight years old, older than some of the kids who were taller than me. Miss Leslie assigned each of us a seat, the smaller ones in the front of the classroom. My desk was in the first row, next to the window, not far from the teacher's big desk.

The mean boys were assigned to the seats in the back of the class. Bill was the name of the biggest boy in the class, but the kids called him Bull. The teacher told us to count from one to twenty-two. At first, we all counted together. Then each of us, in size order, called out our assigned number. Bull made fun of the counting, saying it was baby stuff. He didn't seem to like being last. I saw Grampa whisper to him, and he got quiet.

The teacher told us that it was good that we knew how to count, and that she was going to teach us how to add and subtract. She would teach us the letters, and how to read and write. I thought to myself, "I already know my letters, and how to write them."

The teacher went on talking about classroom *decorum*, a word I had never heard before. Bull and his brothers snickered. Grampa sat down right behind Bull, and he stopped. After a while the teacher said, "Tomorrow we are going to talk about what you did during the summer. Think about what you want to say. Until then, have a good afternoon. Class dismissed. See you tomorrow."

Everyone headed out the door. I waited until the rowdy boys went out the door. Grampa and Miss Leslie were talking at her desk. I walked outside behind some other kids and saw Mama waiting for me.

Then Bull ran by me, hissing, "What's this *colored girl* doing here?"

I saw Mama, and ran over to her, trying hard not to cry. The rowdy boys disappeared down the road. "That big boy called me a colored girl," I whispered to Mama, pointing toward them as they ran away.

"Oh dear," said Mama.

"Why did he say that, Mama? Am I colored?"

"Those are just labels, Willow. We are all human beings."

Grampa came home later that afternoon and told us that he and Miss Leslie had a good conversation. He thought the day had gone well. I told him that Bull said I didn't belong there because I was colored.

The next day, school got worse.

CHAPTER 11

Bullies and Friends

THE SECOND DAY OF SCHOOL started okay. We had a class discussion about what we did over the summer. Miss Leslie told us the rules: "Be quiet when the teacher is speaking. Raise your hand if you want to say something. Only one person talks at a time."

Kids raised their hands, and Miss Leslie called on them, one at a time. Mostly everyone said they helped with farming. Some talked about swimming. A boy named Wilson sat next to me, and he was small like me and limped because he had a clubfoot. Wilson raised his hand, and when Miss Leslie called on him he talked about visiting his cousins up in Tennessee.

I raised my hand to talk about our new farm animals. But Miss Leslie called on Bull, who also had his hand up. Bull did not say what he did over the summer. Instead, he said "Why do you let cripples in your school?" pointing at Wilson.

"Bill," Miss Leslie said, "You do not talk about other children like that!"

"It's a free country, I can say what I want." Bull said, and his brothers snickered.

"Bull—leave this classroom right now!" Miss Leslie ordered, forgetting to call him Bill. Grampa got up and took Bull by the arm to lead him out of the room. Then we went on with the lessons until it was time for dismissal. As I left the schoolhouse, I saw that someone had stomped on all the flowers growing next to the schoolhouse steps.

"Bill is incorrigible," said Grampa at dinner. "I see why people call him *Bull*."

The next morning, there were no rowdy boys in the class. Miss Leslie wrote big letters on the blackboard—A B C D—and handed each of us a booklet and a pencil for us to write down the letters.

I had written A, B, C and was working on D when the three rowdy boys burst into the classroom. Seconds later, their father came through the door. "I took my belt to all of them!" he said to Miss Leslie in a loud voice, and the whole class heard him. "You let me know if they misbehave, and I'll give them another, bigger, whipping!"

I saw Grampa sit down behind Bull.

The rowdy boys' father left the classroom. Miss Leslie handed booklets to the brothers and explained about learning to write the letters.

We went back to writing the letters. Then Bull raised his hand. Miss Leslie called on him. "Teacher, teacher—Gramps here is snoring. We can't hear what you're saying!"

I looked at my Grampa. He was wide awake. He was *not* snoring!

"That's not true, Bill. I expect you—and everyone else—to be respectful in this classroom."

Bull made more snorting sounds, and he saw that everyone was looking at him. Kids giggled, some made snorting noises. Then Miss Leslie stood up from her desk.

"Out of my classroom, Bill!" she commanded.

Bull said, "Come on brothers, let's get out of this stupid school." And they walked out, still snorting.

Miss Leslie muttered under her breath, "backwoods dummies..." All of us in the front row heard her. Nobody said anything. Our teacher was upset, and she dismissed us early.

That afternoon, Miss Leslie quit her teaching job. The Pine Hill School closed until they could hire another teacher. Grampa went to a lot of meetings to try to figure out what to do.

He tried to persuade Miss Leslie to keep her job, but Miss Leslie said she had been trained to never raise her voice while teaching. She told Grampa that she quit because she lost control of the classroom, yelled that day, and said the insulting words, "backwoods dummies." She also told Grampa that she had just graduated from teachers' school and this was her first job.

Grampa told Miss Leslie that everyone makes mistakes, especially when they are new at a job. He thought she could make a good teacher and should try again at Pine Hill School. He said he would write a letter saying what a good job she had been doing, despite a few disruptive students.

Meanwhile, there was no school, and that was fine with me. I stayed home with Mama and played with Molly. The harvest was easier that fall because the Henrys' nephews came up and helped a lot. Our corn crop was plentiful and delicious. Grampa believed his lightning wood had done its job.

Home was better than school, but it wasn't much fun. After the harvest Molly went to visit her cousins in

Birmingham, so there was no one for me to talk to. No new teacher had been hired, and Grampa and Mama knew I would argue if they talked about school.

"I'm bored," I complained at breakfast one morning, yawning.

"Cook with me," said Mama. "We'll make chicken soup and wild-berry pudding." "I don't want to cook," I grumbled. "I just like to eat."

"Then go outside and collect some more kindling for the fireplace," said Grampa.

"I don't want to. The bins are full, and we have enough."

"I'm sick of your whining!" Grampa raised his voice, "I don't care what *you* want. *I'm* trying to read the news-paper." Grampa pointed his finger at me and then at the door. "Go." he said.

That's the way it went after the school shut down. Seemed like both Grampa and Mama wanted me in school just to get me away from them. Everyone was cranky, especially me. I wandered out to my garden. When I felt sad or bored, being in my garden helped. I wondered when Auntie Annie would come. I wanted to see her so bad.

We had another argument at the dinner table. Grampa was late because of yet another school meeting. When he got home, I said to him, "It seems to me that you love that school more than me."

Grampa put his fork down, stared me in the eye, and said, "I love you more than any other child in this world. And that's a big reason why I want this school to work. Pine Hill has been through a lot of hard times, and I want the village to get better, to be more friendly and more educated. Having a community school will help. And it will help you and everyone else who lives here."

"What about Molly? It won't help her—they won't let her in!"

"That's true. That is unfair and terrible. But not going to school won't help. We've got to start somewhere."

A few weeks went by. Then after supper one night, Grampa asked me and Mama a question, "Would it be okay to invite a few friends over?"

"Who?" said Mama.

"Miss Leslie and Mr. Luke," said Grampa. "You mean Miss Leslie, my teacher?" I asked. "Yes, your school teacher."

"I like Miss Leslie," I said quietly.

"Mr. Luke, the man who built the school, also wants to come over," Grampa said. Then he turned to me. "Willow, I've kept your secret. But some people at the groundbreaking saw those boys attack you. Mr. Luke's children saw them knock you over. Mr. Luke wants to hear your story from you."

"Who are Mr. Luke's kids?"

"Let's see if I remember their names: Cindy, David, Janice, Tommy, and Wilson."

"Wilson? The boy with the clubfoot?"

"That's the one."

"I like those kids." So I agreed that Grampa could invite Miss Leslie and Mr. Luke to visit us.

A week later, Miss Leslie, Mr. Luke, and Wilson all came over. We all sat around our big table—Grampa at one end, and Miss Leslie at the other end. Mr. Luke and his son, Wilson, sat on one side of the table. I sat on the other side, next to the wall. I hoped Mama would sit down next to me. But Mama served us tea and cake and then went back in the kitchen. I could see her from where I sat, and I knew she was listening.

Miss Leslie asked me to tell what happened to me. I told them my story, how—every time I was around Bull—he and his brothers would push me, knock me down, call me names, and say that I didn't belong at the school. "One of them said, *You're dead!*"

Next Wilson told us how he felt when Bull called him a cripple. "I can run," said Wilson, "probably faster than Bull can."

Then Miss Leslie said, "I have something to say as well. I made a big mistake that day. It is my job to keep order in the classroom. And when Bill was cutting up, it upset me so much that I lost my decorum and said something I deeply regret."

Miss Leslie looked at me, "Do you remember what I said?" I replied, "Yes. You said, 'backwoods dummies.'"

Wilson looked at Miss Leslie and added, "I heard you say it--you were right! Those boys *are* dummies!"

Then Miss Leslie said, "No, Wilson, I should never have said those words. It insults everyone who lives in the woods, and a lot of good people live in the woods. It was wrong. I've talked with Mr. Luke and Mr. Jones about it. They tell me that if I talk to people and apologize that maybe I can keep teaching at Pine Hill School."

Then Miss Leslie looked at me, "Willow, what do you think?"

"I think you are a good teacher and that Bull was really bad that day," I said. "He also lied about my Grampa snoring! I won't go to that school if Bull is there."

"Well, I have some news to report," said Miss Leslie. "Bill has been dismissed from Pine Hill School for disrespecting adults and threatening children. We are reopening Pine Hill School in two weeks, on November 1. But Bill is not allowed to come near the school.

"Will you join us to try again to have school?" Miss Leslie asked. "Your Grampa will continue to be my assistant. I hope both of you, Willow and Wilson, will come back to school. What do you say, Wilson?"

"Yes—I'll come back to school," said Wilson happily. "What do you say, Willow?"

"Maybe," I mumbled. "There is something I want to say. I don't think it's fair that Negro children aren't allowed to go to Pine Hill School."

"Oh," said Miss Leslie, "I didn't know there were Negro children living here."

"My best friend, Molly, lives here. She is a teenager and is so smart that she already knows everything you are teaching us. She would make a great teacher, but she can't even go to the school or to the public library."

"Molly sounds like a wonderful young woman," said Miss Leslie. "Maybe you could introduce her to me sometime."

Then our visitors got ready to leave. Before she left, Miss Leslie went into the kitchen to speak to Mama, and I heard them laughing. I liked that. People often ignore my mama because she is shy and sad. But Miss Leslie was nice, and it was good to hear Mama laugh.

CHAPTER 12

Secret Grandmother

I HADN'T YET DECIDED FOR myself if I was going back to the Pine Hill School. I knew Grampa and Mama wanted me to go. The days grew shorter and the mornings colder. One morning I wandered to my garden, a good place to go when I felt sad or lonely. I kept thinking about my Auntie. She hadn't come to visit this fall, even though the harvest was over and it sure felt like frost was on its way.

"Where is Auntie?" I wondered. "I want so badly to see her, talk to her." The wind picked up. The trees were swaying and clouds covered the sun.

"Willow," Mama called, "Storm's coming. Time to come inside."

"I'll come in if it starts raining," I answered. I walked down to the road and looked north, as far up the road as I could see. There, in the distance, someone was walking with a cane, wearing a long skirt and old shawl that blew to one side like the wing of an injured bird. It was Auntie, heading towards me.

I ran all the way to her. "Auntie, I'm so glad you're here—been thinking about you!" "This wind's been pushing me to you," she said, "To my Willow in the winds."

The rain began, lightly at first, and we moved as fast as we could towards the shelter of the house. Then the heavens let loose, and Auntie grabbed my hand and we ran for the porch.

"Thank you, rain!" Auntie shouted, still holding my hand. I noticed how brown we both were, browned by the sun.

Mama opened the front door and brought us quickly into the house. She took us into her bedroom and put warm, dry blankets around us—and took our sopping wet clothing from us. Grampa built a fire in the big fireplace. We sat down in the rocking chairs, wrapped in blankets, in front of the blaze.

"Auntie, you must stay for supper, and overnight," said Grampa.

"So your clothes can dry," added Mama, heading up to the attic to hang our wet clothes on a clothesline up there.

"Thank you. This fire sure feels good," answered Auntie. After pausing a bit, she said, "I accept your hospitality. I don't want to get a chill."

The next day, it poured, and that's why we got Auntie to stay with us for two nights and three days. She slept in my room, and I slept on a palette on the living room floor.

We had to stay inside because of the stormy weather. Grampa and Auntie spoke in words I didn't know. "We're talking Chickasaw," Grampa said. Then he talked with words I did know, explaining how he learned fire-making and hunting from his Chickasaw friends.

Auntie said she wished there were more, good white folks like Grampa and Mama. She talked about how sad it was when the Chickasaws and other Indian people were forced to go west. She told us how she lived in her family's village, hidden up in the mountains.

I loved hearing her stories. I helped Mama cook dinner, and we sat around and talked till bedtime. Grampa bragged about me learning my letters and numbers. Auntie said, "Good for you, Willow."

The next morning was Sunday, and Grampa went with Mama to church. That left me and Auntie alone by the fireplace, sipping mint tea and eating biscuits with mint jelly. Then the sun came out, making it beautiful outside. We wandered through the garden and fields.

"Would you like me to tell you a story?" asked Auntie. "Yes! Please tell me a story."

We sat down on the bench in the sunshine. Auntie cleared her throat and began.

"Once upon a time, a sweet little baby was born in a beautiful village in the mountains. She lived with her mother and grandmother who loved her very much. She loved to play in the meadow and wander in the cornfield. She tried to help her mama with the farming."

I closed my eyes and lay down across Auntie's lap.

"Then one day, her mama went into town. Some very terrible men hurt her—hurt her real bad. The mama had to leave this earth and go up in the sky to the spirit world."

"This is a sad story!" I whispered. I kept my eyes closed. I heard Auntie weeping.

After a few moments, Auntie continued. "The grandmother loved the little girl so much, and she tried to take care of her. But times were hard, and there wasn't enough food to eat. So the grandmother looked for another mommy to look after her grandbaby. She found Mama Red Bud and Grampa Joe, and she gave her little granddaughter to them. The baby grew into a little girl, and then she got bigger and bigger. Mama Red Bud and Grampa Joe loved her very much. And that's my story."

I didn't want the story to stop. But Auntie had stopped talking.

I opened my eyes, and looked up, "Is that story about me?" "Yes, it is about you," said Auntie, wiping tears from her eyes.

I sat up, and asked more questions. "Does that mean I am Chickasaw?"

"Yes," whispered Auntie, "I am your Chickasaw grandmother, and I love you very much."

Then Auntie--I mean, Grandmother—pulled something wrapped in a cloth out of her shoulder bag. Carefully, she put it in my hand. It was a hair comb made out of bone with a little blue jay carved on it.

"It's beautiful!" I said.

"Long ago, my father carved it for my mother, whose name was Tishkila, which means *blue jay* in Chickasaw. I am giving it to you, to help you remember your roots."

I sat there next to my grandmother, holding the beautiful comb that my great grandfather made for my great grandmother. For a time, we were quiet—just my very own Chickasaw grandmother and me. It felt so peaceful. Then I went to my room to hide this comb in a special secret place.

Quickly I came back outside to Auntie—I mean, Grandmother. She said to me. "Don't tell your Mama Rose or your Grampa that I told you all this. Let it be our secret."

"I promise to keep it secret," I said. I needed to be careful to keep Auntie's secret, but I smiled to myself, because she was my real grandmother.

"I sure wish I was living up in that village with you."

"You have a good home here, Willow," Grandmother said. "Your Mama Rose and Grampa love you very much. And I will keep coming to see you as long as I'm able. I will keep telling you stories, so you can learn your Chickasaw heritage."

I thought of another, more pressing, question to ask my grandmother. "Grampa and Mama Rose want me to go to school—but I hate that school!" I told her about the mean boys calling me *colored* and saying I didn't belong in the school. I held my arm up to hers and told my real grandmother that I could see that we were the same color. I said, "We're colored like Molly and her folks, even though we are different colors." And I told her that Molly and her parents couldn't go to the library or the school. I went on and on.

"Goodness, you have a lot to say for a small girl!" my grandmother said, "But I agree with Mama Rose and Grampa. You *should* go to school. Learn what you can. Reading and writing is important for all people—Indian, Negro, and white. The children in my village are going to the new public school near us. It's supposed to be a "white" school, but half of the students there got Indian in them!"

"I just want to learn about the Chickasaws," I declared.

Then Grandmother said, "I've something very important to tell you. I *love* being Chickasaw, but I have to be careful because it's illegal to be Indian here since the tribes got forced out."

Sighing, she added, "Be proud you are an Indian, Willow, but be careful who you tell. When you were a baby, when I gave you to Grampa Jack and Mama Rose,

I asked them to *raise you as a white girl*. And they promised to do that. So don't go around announcing that you are Indian, 'cause it could get you into trouble."

Then she took my hands and looked into my eyes. "Keep calling me Auntie," my grandmother told me. "It's our secret that I am your grandmother."

My Chickasaw grandmother stayed in my thoughts after she left. And in the years to come she kept her promise, visiting me every fall and telling me stories about people in her village.

After she left, there were only a few days before Pine Hill School reopened. I thought about going to that school. I liked Miss Leslie, and most important, Bull would not be there. But I still worried. What if Bull lurked around the school—or in the nearby woods, and went after me when school let out? I couldn't stop thinking about that.

Two days before the school reopened, Grampa sat down to supper, and said, "Guess who I saw today?"

"Who?" I asked.

"George Sawyer, who cut down the trees for us. Do you remember the names of the Sawyers' daughters?"

"Yes," I said, "Sue Ann, Clara Louise, and Peggy Lynn. We had fun playing together."

"Well, guess who is going to Pine Hill School? And guess who needs to come to breakfast on the day school reopens?"

"The three Sawyer girls?" I asked.

"Yes! The Sawyer brothers need to drop their daughters off here so they can go to work. And before dinner, they will pick them up here. Won't be every day, but it will be often."

Sue Ann's and Peggy Lynn's mother was Chickasaw, and I remembered how much fun me and Molly had playing with them while their dads cut down trees.

"That settles it!" I announced to Grampa and Mama, "I'll go to Pine Hill School with my friends the Sawyer girls!"

On November 1, 1875, I walked to Pine Hill School with my three friends.

"Shhhh....," said Sue Ann as we started down the road. "It's a secret. We're Indians--we look out for each other." And then we were quiet for a few steps and then started giggling. We laughed, ran through the leaves, and played tag.

We got to school on time. School was okay, sometimes it was even fun. Having friends made a big difference. Playing with my three girl-friends was great—everyone in the class knew that if they messed with any one of us, all of us would fight them. We were tough, and no one bothered us.

I went to that school for four years, and I learned to read and write. When Sue Ann and I turned twelve, we finished Pine Hill School. I figured we had learned all we needed to know.

CHAPTER 13

Thomas' Plantation

W HEN MY BEST FRIEND MOLLY turned thirteen, she told me, "I am no longer a child, I'm coming of age." I was just seven when Molly and my brother Thomas both turned thirteen. I learned a lot from them about "coming of age." They seemed to go crazy, each in their own way.

When Thomas was thirteen, he came up to our house for Christmas—grumpy and complaining. Thomas spent three days with us, letting us know he hated every minute of it. He complained about how poor we were, criticized our chipped dinner plates, and beat-up furniture. Most of all, he complained about how cold our house was.

"We do the best we can, Grandson," said Grampa. "Very few people are rich like your Uncle Andrew. Most folks have to work hard to eat and stay warm. If you are cold, go put on the long johns I gave you for Christmas."

"I don't like long johns," Thomas grumbled.

"Then go get more wood from the woodshed and build up the fire in the fireplace."

But Thomas didn't want to get wood—he wanted a servant to do his bidding. I was counting the hours until Thomas went back to Birmingham.

I escaped to Molly's house, and she showed me her Christmas present, a book called *My Bondage, My Freedom.* "It's written by Frederick Douglass, himself," she told me. "He tells the truth about what's right and what's wrong. It's a great book and I'm going to read every page of it."

Molly wanted to come over to my house to say "Hi," to Thomas, who was her "friend from birth." She had not seen him in a long time, and lots had changed. Molly told me some stories about things she and Thomas did together when they were little, like stealing cookies from Miz Mildred's cookie jar.

As we went into the house, we saw Thomas and Mama in the kitchen. Mama was putting a plate of food in front of her son. Thomas sat at the kitchen table with a rude face, looking like a little king.

Thomas looked up at Molly and me and sneered at us. Then he growled to Mama, "What kind of white trash family is this? A savage Injun girl? Dirty nigras living next door?"

I couldn't believe my ears—Thomas insulting us! I knew I had to speak, and loud words flew out of my mouth, *"Thomas, you cannot say bad things about our mother and my best friend!"*

Mama looked at me, then at her son. She quickly picked up the plate of food she had just put in front of Thomas. She opened the cupboard behind her, put that plate on the shelf, closed the door, and stood blocking the cupboard, her arms akimbo.

"Mama, give me my food!" Thomas shouted.

"Not until you apologize, young man!" Mama told him. "You are not allowed to say hateful things in this house!"

Thomas suddenly realized he was outnumbered by the three females he had just insulted. He crumbled in front of us, putting his head down on his arms on the table. I saw him whimper.

Then Grampa appeared in the doorway. He walked over to Thomas, put his hands on his grandson's shoulders, saying, "Thomas, let's go talk." Thomas stood up without looking at any of us and followed Grampa out of the room.

Why did Grampa take him away? I wanted to yell at Thomas some more. "He's learning to be hateful at that fancy boarding school," I grumbled to Mama and Molly. I was furious. I went to bed that night wondering why Thomas could say such nasty things about us. *White trash family? Savage Injun girl? Dirty nigras?* It reminded me of those bullies at school.

Thomas never said he was sorry—to me, or to Molly. I don't know if he apologized to Mama. The next morning, I looked in the cupboard for that plate of chicken dumplings, green beans, and cornbread. It was gone. Mama or Grampa must have given it to him last night. Or maybe he stole it out of our cupboard. I was furious at Thomas. But I realized that Grampa and Mama still loved him, even though he was so mean and selfish.

The next morning, Grampa took Thomas to Market Town to catch the public coach to Birmingham. I helped Mama in the kitchen. Mama told me she was a failure as a mother. She was appalled that her own son could say those nasty words.

"Mama," I said, "I think you are a great mom."

Mama mumbled, talking to herself, "How can I put this? I just got to open my mouth, let it come out." I quietly watched Mama struggle with herself. Then she looked at me, and said clearly, "I am proud of you for telling Thomas not to insult us."

She took my hand, saying, "Ever since I was a little girl, I've been taught to be quiet. *Girls are to be seen but not heard*—that's what my mother and grandmother taught me. Men, white men, make the decisions. They make the speeches, become the leaders. Women are only allowed to take care of the children—feed the family. That's what I learned as a child."

Mama poured tea for both of us. "Yesterday," she said, "after Thomas called us a white-trash family, I was still planning to feed him his supper. That was my role— feed him, don't criticize him. Then you and Molly came in, and you spoke the truth. I thought, Willow is right! I can't just feed him when he talks like that."

Mama paused, "I want you to know that Thomas' father–my dear husband–*would never talk like that!* He must be rolling over in his grave, his son saying those things."

Later I talked to Grampa about Thomas' nasty mouth. Grampa stoked up the fire in the fireplace and sat down in his easy chair. "Thomas, Jr. is growing up as a rich white boy on a plantation. I wish he was more like his father, who left that plantation to join us in opposing slavery. I wish that my grandson had grown up in *this* house with *us*."

Grampa told me how bad words like that make people feel angry and lead to fights. "It's worse for colored people, because white people say those mean things to colored people, knowing they can get away with it because they are white. If a colored person gets angry, and says or does anything, white people can hurt—or even kill—him. Violence against the colored happens all too often, and whites are never punished."

A few days later, on a mild, sunny winter day, Molly and I wandered around our fields. I told Molly what Grampa told me. Molly agreed, saying, "That's why Frederick Douglass is so important. He is a colored man who speaks out. He gives speeches!"

But then Molly pointed out something I had not thought of. "Thomas is coming of age, like me," she said, "and when kids come of age, they get angry. Thomas is angry, and I'm angry, too. But at least I know that my mother and father love me. Thomas never had a daddy, and he went away to school when he was only eight. Now he is thirteen and he doesn't hardly know his mother and grandfather."

Molly paused, and we wandered to the pond. "I watch the way Thomas looks at you," Molly said. "He's jealous of you, Willow. You have his mother's love around you all the time. And he doesn't."

The following year, Thomas' Uncle Andrew and Aunt Frida invited us to join them for Christmas at their plantation home in Birmingham. Mama was all excited about it, and I got excited too. Molly loved Birmingham, and I thought maybe I would too. But I *hated* it! Birmingham is a big place, and on that trip I did not see the Birmingham that Molly loved. I only saw this big, fancy plantation where Thomas lived with his snobby uncle, aunt, and two teenaged boy cousins.

We planned to leave for Birmingham at dawn on Christmas Eve and get there in time for dinner. Then a bracket on our buggy broke, and Grampa had to repair it before we could travel. That meant we got a late start and we got there too late for Christmas Eve dinner.

It was dark when our horse and buggy finally pulled up in front of an enormous white house. I had never seen a house that big for one family. It looked bigger than the fancy hotel in Market Town. The people who met us at the door were all colored and wearing uniforms.

"Welcome to the Fields Plantation," one of them said.

I had not yet met my Uncle Andrew or Aunt Frida, and all the people welcoming us were colored. "Are Aunt and Uncle colored?" I whispered to Mama.

"No," she whispered to me. "These are their servants. Rich people show how rich they are by having lots of servants dressed in uniforms."

One man took Sugar and our buggy, and another ushered us through the elegant front door into a huge room with a very high ceiling. A wide staircase in front of us curved up to the floor high above us. Another lady in uniform welcomed us and introduced herself as Annie Mae.

She told us, "Dinner is over, but if you are hungry, we can feed you in the kitchen."

We were hungry! Thank goodness they could feed us. After the buggy broke down, I wasn't sure we'd *ever* eat. We followed Annie Mae to a big kitchen, where she seated us at a wooden table in the corner. The kitchen was the biggest one I'd ever seen, but not fancy like the rest of the house.

Annie Mae introduced us to Lila, the cook, who served us dinner. Lila gave us leftovers from the supper we had missed, apologizing for not seating us in the dining room. She said that room was being cleaned for Christmas breakfast.

"That suits us just fine," Grampa told Lila.

Mama said that she loved eating in this kitchen. "I've spent my whole life cooking in my own little kitchen," she said. As we ate our supper, we watched the women preparing the next day's Christmas feast.

Our supper was good, and we were tired. After we finished, Annie Mae reappeared and took us up to our bedrooms on the second floor. Grampa had a room to himself, and Mama and I shared the fanciest bedroom I'd ever seen. We each had a big double bed to ourselves, and there was a dressing area with a big closet, and what Annie Mae called a *water closet* with a chamber pot, a basin, and jugs of water ready for us to use.

I fell asleep as soon as I hit the pillow, and next thing I knew it was morning. While we were dressing we heard the bell ring announcing that breakfast was served. We made our way down to the massive dining room, where Grampa introduced me to Aunt Frida and Uncle Andrew. When Thomas and his two cousins arrived a few minutes later, we sat down around the huge dining room table.

There were lots of fancy plates and glasses. "A full setting of fine china and silverware," Mama whispered to me. I'd heard the word "silverware" before, but had never seen anything made of silver.

The servants served the breakfast. I watched Aunt Frida as she turned up her nose at a covered platter of scrambled eggs, saying the eggs were "too cold." Lila took the platter back to the kitchen. Those eggs looked good to me, and they weren't cold—I could see the heat steaming off them.

My brother Thomas and his cousins, Andrew Jr. and Matthew, sat opposite Mama, Grampa, and me. They whispered to each other, snickering about something. Was it about me? I wondered. They reminded me of the mean boys at my school.

After breakfast, people gathered in the living room, where there was a huge Christmas tree with presents under it. Mama asked me to put the gifts we brought under the tree. They were jars of Mama's best home-made grape preserves from our own grapevines, and they were wrapped in pretty, store-bought Christmas paper. I watched Aunt Frida take the wrapping off one jar. She hardly looked at it, and ordered one of the servants to take all the jars to the kitchen. Grampa's present for Thomas was a new tie. When Thomas unwrapped it, he laughed and tossed the tie aside.

Aunt Frida called to Thomas, and gave him a tiny box to bring it to me. I opened it and there was a little silver necklace with a Christmas tree on it. Mama helped me put it around my neck. And then I went over to thank Aunt Frida.

Mama whispered to me, "At least one child here has good manners," adding that she wished my big brother was as well-behaved as I was.

Finally, Uncle Andrew announced that he and *his boys* would give us a tour of the estate. We put on our coats and hats, and followed him as he showed off the farm and cotton fields. Colored people were everywhere, working. I wondered, why they didn't get a day off for Christmas? But I kept quiet. Uncle Andrew bragged that his house had over forty rooms in it and sat on five hundred acres of farm land.

Lunch was served buffet style in another big room called the Day Room. Thomas and his cousins started cutting up, talking loud and disrespectful. Aunt Frida told them, "Children should be seen and not heard." The three boys laughed at her, and her husband told the boys to be quiet or leave the room. They gobbled down some lunch and then left, making much commotion.

"Where have I gone wrong?" Aunt Frida whispered to Mama, who was sitting next to Mama and me. Mama whispered in Aunt Frida's ear something that made my aunt laugh. After we finished eating, we were told that it was rest time, and that Christmas Dinner would be served in the dining room. When we got to our room, Mama lay down and went to sleep.

I wasn't tired, so I tiptoed out of our room and wandered around the huge house. I walked up the curved staircase to the top. But some servants were doing something up there, and they frowned at me and told me to go back downstairs. I decided to go to the kitchen, where the friendly women were cooking dinner. I said hello to Lila, who had served us food the night before. I asked if I could help her, and she let me follow her as she opened the door to a big storage closet. She told me I could help her get plates and silverware ready for dinner. Then I asked if they got any time off for themselves at Christmas. "No," she replied. "But the day after tomorrow is Sunday, our day off."

We were in the storage closet, counting out the silverware, when suddenly there was a loud cry—a howl of pain. A girl, not much bigger than me, ran through the door into the kitchen, calling, "Mama!" She saw Lila and me in the storage room. Lila almost dropped the dinner plates as she grabbed her sobbing daughter. I stood there silently behind Lila as she closed the storage-room door with her foot and hugged her child.

"Hannah, what happened?" Lila asked her daughter.

"The overseer..." Hannah cried. Lila gently removed her daughter's cape, and I saw blood seeping from Hannah's back through her dress. Lila gently enveloped her daughter, who continued to sob.

Then Lila looked up and saw me. "Claudette!" she called out, and another woman opened the storage-room door. "Take this child back to her room."

And, wordlessly, Claudette took my hand, and led me to a narrow servant's staircase that led upstairs.

"What happened?" I asked Claudette as we climbed the steep stairs.

"Oh, child," Claudette said to me, "Nothing you need to worry about." She quickly took me to the room I shared with Mama, and left me there.

I saw Mama sleeping as I opened the door and tiptoed in. Suddenly, I felt sick and ran to the water closet and threw up in the chamber pot. Then I lay down in my bed, remembering the blood on that girl's back. When Lila had asked her daughter, "What happened?" the girl had said something I had never heard before. Was it "over see her" or "over to see her"? Who did she go over to see?

Who could I talk to? I knew I couldn't tell Mama or Grampa about it because they would get angry about me wandering around where I shouldn't be. They might even tell Uncle Andrew, and it could turn into a big mess. I decided to wait and talk to Miz Mildred about it. She would tell me and keep it secret.

I wanted to get out of Birmingham. Instead I had to lie there, smelling the throw-up in the chamber pot. When Mama woke up, she too smelled my throw-up. I told her I felt sick. I was glad I didn't have to go down for dinner.

The next morning there was a buffet breakfast. I did not eat anything or say a word. Nobody noticed me. I just watched people and wondered what kind of folks could harm a young girl? My cousins and my big brother whispered and laughed. I wondered if those boys had anything to do with hurting that girl.

We left for home right after breakfast. "What a nice visit," Mama said as we drove away. Then she asked me, "Did you enjoy yourself?" I nodded, and looked out across the fields and woods, wondering why that girl had blood on her back.

We got home that night. The next day, I went to see Miz Mildred. She was alone in her house because Molly was in Birmingham and Mr. Henry was working in Market Town. "Miz Mildred, I want to ask you about something I saw in Birmingham. I can't talk to Mama or Grampa about it. It's a secret. Can you keep it secret?"

Mildred looked at me. "Not if you did something you shouldn't have done." "No, it's *not* something I did. It is something *I saw*. And I don't understand it." "Okay—then tell me."

I told her about being in the kitchen and seeing the girl with the blood on her back. Mildred asked me some questions, and I answered her as best I could. I told her the girl said something about "over see her." Miz Mildred thought for a moment. Then she said, "Overseer." She explained that on all plantations there is an *overseer* who is the boss of the people who work in the fields. "The overseer punishes the colored people by whipping them," Miz Mildred told me. "My guess is that girl had blood on her back because the overseer whipped her."

"Why would the overseer do that?" I asked.

"Overseers are always mean. It is their job. The over-seer has to make people afraid of him. That's how he makes people work hard for little or nothing. He whips a person who doesn't work fast enough—or who refuses to do what he tells them to do—or takes something they shouldn't take. It's also possible that the overseer whipped her just because he felt like it." Miz Mildred paused and frowned. Then she said, "Slavery is supposed to be gone. But, for a lot of folks, what we got now ain't any better."

I thought about what Mildred said. "I hate where Thomas lives," I told her. "I will never go back to that plantation again!"

Miz Mildred handed me a piece of pumpkin pie, and I ate it. "There's something else I hate," I said. "My last name is 'Fields.' I don't want that last name."

"Not much you can do about your last name until you marry," commented Miz Mildred. "Besides, generally, *fields* are good. We live off of our corn*fields*."

I still hated having Fields as my last name.

I kept my word. I never went back to the Fields Plantation. Thomas refused to come to see us, but over the years Grampa and Mama went to see him several times in Birmingham. Then Thomas moved even farther south to Montgomery, the state capital, to study law. My brother Thomas remained a stranger to me for the rest of my life.

CHAPTER 14

The Election of 1876

IN SCHOOL, MISS LESLIE TAUGHT us history. But she never talked about Frederick Douglass. I think that was because my school was a *white* school, colored not allowed. I was lucky to have Molly teach me about Frederick Douglass.

Sometimes we had arguments in school, especially during the fall when I was nine. Miss Leslie taught us that that the United States of America was born in 1776. "Now it is 1876, and our country is one hundred years old," she said. She taught us about the Declaration of Independence and the American Revolution. We had a big argument in class about whether "all people are created equal." When we talked about the Civil War, there was some more shouting in the classroom. Miss Leslie said we needed to keep our decorum.

That November there was a presidential election. Miss Leslie taught us that the two candidates for president were Rutherford B. Hayes, the Republican, and Samuel Tilden, the Democrat. Only adult men could vote. "It used to be only white men could vote," she said, "But six years ago, in 1870, the United States government decided that colored men could also vote."

"Why aren't colored children allowed in our school?" I asked. That touched off another big argument. "Of course, they can't come to this school," one boy said, "they are slow."

"They can't learn like us," another boy said.

I kept saying, "That's not true! That's not true!" It was a big debate, and it led to all kinds of yelling. Miss Leslie dismissed the class early. I was especially glad to have three girlfriends to walk home with after school that day.

On another day, we had a class discussion about whether women should be allowed to vote. Some girls, including me, said women should vote. But the preacher's daughter, Lilly Ann, said, "Women's role is in the home, not in politics." Then my friend Sue Ann raised her hand and said, "Girls are as smart as boys! We should be allowed to vote." Some of us girls clapped for her. But the boys thought girls should never vote.

Then Miss Leslie told us we would have a class discussion about the 1876 candidates for president, Hayes and Tilden. She chose the two smartest boys in the class, George and Daryl. They were supposed to find out about the two candidates and report to the class. After school, Miss Leslie met with George and Daryl. As I left the school house, I heard Miss Leslie tell those boys that that their presentations should be *dignified*.

Well, they were *not* dignified—and it became another big squabble. George supported Rutherford B Hayes, because he said all the smart people knew Hayes would bring the South out of poverty. But Daryl said, "Hogwash! Hayes is a *nigra-lover*! He will *never* get elected!" Some kids started yelling and saying bad words. Miss Leslie quickly dismissed the class.

The next day was Election Day. I saw Grampa getting ready to vote, putting on his best Sunday suit even though it was Tuesday. Grampa said, "Mr. Henry and I are going to go cast our votes for president of the United States."

"Who are you voting for, Grampa?" I asked him.

"Rutherford B. Hayes," he said, "because he has opposed slavery for his whole life and he fought for the Union in the Civil War."

Mr. Henry came over and I asked him who he was voting for. "Rutherford B. Hayes," he said, "I hope he will help the colored. Tilden will do nothing because the Democrat Party down here in the South wants to keep colored people down." And off they went to vote in Market Town.

The next day, I asked Grampa, "Who won?"

"We don't know. They got to count the votes first," he said. Every day, I asked him who had won, and every day, Grampa told me to be patient—it takes a while to count votes. It took months and months.

One night that winter, Molly invited us over for dinner. She told me, "My dad will tell us what he thinks about voting." I was happy that Mr. Henry wanted to talk to us.

After dinner and cleanup, Mr. Henry said, "I lived during slavery and through the Civil War, and I want to tell you some things I learned." Molly, Grampa, and I sat down to listen. Mama and Miz Mildred excused themselves to make pies for the Pine Hill Grocery.

"When the North won the War in 1865, I got my hopes up," Mr. Henry told us. "All of us colored folks got our hopes up. Slavery was over! We were free! We were American citizens with rights! But we colored people *never* had a chance. Many people left the plantations to get away from the slave masters. But they needed to feed themselves.

"Then, in 1866—just a year after the war ended—the Alabama State Legislature passed a Vagrancy Law that said if you were colored and didn't have a job you were breaking the law. Punishment for a colored man or woman breaking that law was *thirty-nine lashes on your bare back!* The Vagrancy Law meant colored people had to go back to the plantation and work for the men who used to own them. If they didn't work, they would get whipped and thrown in jail and forced to work on a chain gang. Some freedom! And all the southern states passed laws like that. They called them Black Codes. The national government did nothing about it."

I shivered as Mr. Henry spoke, remembering the blood on the back of the girl at the Fields Plantation.

"After the Civil War," Mr. Henry continued, "lots of good-hearted men and women came down from the North to help us. Both colored people and whites came to teach us to read and write and to help us exercise our rights. Then suddenly, the Ku Klux Klan started killing people, especially our colored leaders, and also the northerners who were trying to help us. They burned down people's homes, shot people, and scared everybody. The South became very dangerous for colored people and their friends.

"Up in the North, the government passed these high-sounding Amendments to the Constitution. The Thirteenth Amendment ended slavery, the Fourteenth Amendment gave us equal rights, and the Fifteenth Amendment gave voting rights for all men, black and white. But it was all just spit and shine. The plantation owners used violence and the Ku Klux Klan to get around those Amendments. They held elections, but they had already decided who would win. Now they're still strutting sitting down."

Mr. Henry wiped his brow, and stopped for a break. Miz Mildred served us cake. I could hardly eat the cake—I wanted Mr. Henry to keep talking.

"Six years ago," Mr. Henry said, wiping cake crumbs off his mouth, "the US passed the Fifteenth Amendment, which gave colored men the right to vote. It was 1870, and there was a close race for Alabama governor that year. A big colored vote could mean Alabama would elect a governor who was more friendly towards the colored race. But right before the election, the KKK killed five black men! And on election morning, they shot some colored men who were just lining up to vote. People got scared. Who wanted to risk their lives just to cast a vote? And the Southern white racists won that election.

"That's the way it went. Four years later, in 1874, there was another close election. In Greene County, Alabama—not far from the Mississippi border where I was born—colored men stood in line to vote. White men opened fire on them, shooting *more than a hundred colored men!* The United States Army was stationed nearby—but they did *nothing* to help the people.

"That's my story," Mr. Henry concluded. "The North won the war, but it hasn't meant a hill of beans to poor black folks. I'm lucky to still be alive, could've died any number of times."

I went home that night, thinking about what Mr. Henry had said. It made me mad. He explained it so clearly—he should be a teacher. It was unfair that neither he nor Molly could go to my school. The next day, I thanked Mr.

Henry for talking to us and said, "I wish you could talk to my class at Pine Hill School."

"They won't let me in the door," whispered Mr. Henry. "And if I did get in, some white crackers might catch me and hang me from the bridge."

"That's terrible!" I cried.

"It's an unfair world, Willow." Mr. Henry responded. "We just got to do the best we can. Thank goodness we have each other right here in Pine Hill. Molly wants to move away, but I tell you, in my mind we're lucky to live right here."

Back at school, we kept asking Miss Leslie when they would finish counting the vote for president. She told us about something called "electoral votes" that were so complicated that even Miss Leslie didn't understand it. That 1876 election wasn't decided until 1877! Tilden had won the popular vote, but not the electoral vote, so the government said no one had won the presidency. Then the government made a deal with Rutherford B. Hayes. If he agreed to end Reconstruction by pulling the US Army out of the South, and then he would get the electoral votes to become president! They called it the Compromise of 1877.

"Disgusting!" said Grampa. "Rutherford B. Hayes is a liar! He ran for president standing for reconstructing the South for all the people. Then he sold out and gave the plantation owners what they wanted. And that's how he got elected."

"Yup," added Mr. Henry. "The big wigs and their politicians always find a way to get what they want. That's how they keep us all down."

I soon forgot about the Compromise of 1877. There were more important things happening in our lives.

CHAPTER 15

Molly's Birmingham

WHEN MOLLY TURNED FOURTEEN, SHE told me she was old enough to make up her own mind—and she wanted to get out of Pine Hill. She argued with her parents all the time. She never became hateful like Thomas, but she certainly expressed her anger. Her hero was Frederick Douglass, whose book she read cover-to-cover. "When Frederick Douglass sees something wrong," she told me, "he gives speeches."

We celebrated Molly's fourteenth birthday at the Henrys' house. Miz Mildred roasted a chicken and potatoes, and Mama baked a chocolate birthday cake. We enjoyed the delicious dinner and were getting ready to eat cake. Then Molly stood up. "I turned fourteen today, and that means I am pretty much grown." Dramatically, she looked at each of us. "I love you all, but *I want to get out of this place*!"

"Molly, sit down." ordered Mr. Henry.

"It's my birthday," protested Molly, ignoring her father. "Like Frederick Douglass, I'm gonna have my say."

Raising her voice, Molly looked at her father, "Do you know we are the only Negro people for miles around? Most of our family left here along with all the other colored folks. They went to cities like Birmingham and Chicago. I wish we had moved out of here."

Molly took a deep breath, "There is *nothing in this place for me!* I can't go to school, can't go to the library, can't go here, can't go there. I can't go anywhere except on Sunday when we travel to our colored church. That's the only time I have fun."

Molly turned and looked at me and my folks, saying, "I *love* you—Willow, Grampa, and Miz Rose—but all the other white folks 'round here hate colored people. You know how they do. And I hate them back."

Molly put her hand on Grampa's shoulder. "Thank you, Grampa, for borrowing that library book for me, *Birmingham: City of Progress.* That book taught me a lot. I learned that *white people don't think there are any colored people in Birmingham!* That book is full of drawings of people—building this and leading that. None of them are colored except for one maid serving her master his dinner. Anyone with eyesight can see that there are lots of colored people in Birmingham. My cousins go to schools and libraries that are just for the colored. I want to stay down there with them, but Mama and Papa won't let me."

Molly's parents looked shocked. My mama had a funny look on her face. Maybe she realized that Thomas wasn't the only sassy child.

Grampa stood up, saying, "Coming of age is hard for young'uns, and perhaps even harder for their parents. We are going to leave y'all to sort this one out. Thank you for the delicious dinner, Miz Mildred." Grampa took my hand, and we went back to our house, leaving that chocolate birthday cake sitting there on the table.

That whole spring, Molly argued with her parents. Several times when I went to their house, Miz Mildred met me at the door to tell me Molly could not see me that day because she was being punished. Eventually, the Henrys came to a compromise. Based on good behavior, Molly could spend one week every month with her cousins in Birmingham.

"I learned one thing," Molly told me when she came back from a trip to Birmingham. "When you come of age, you can say *no* to the things you really don't like. I didn't get everything I wanted, but I got to have some good times in Birmingham."

As the years went on, based on good behavior, Molly spent more and more time in Birmingham. The main time I spent with her was during the growing season, when we weeded the cornfields. I missed Molly. Fortunately, I was still in school with my friends Sue Ann, Clara Louise, and Peggy Lynn.

Molly became an expert on Frederick Douglass. Her cousin, Stella, a teacher in Birmingham's colored public school, asked Molly to come to her classroom and talk about Mr. Douglass.

Molly practiced giving her Frederick Douglass talk to me, pretending I was one of Stella's pupils. I got to ask questions, and learned a lot.

The next year, Molly studied Harriet Tubman, who was "the Moses of her people." During slavery times, she led hundreds of people out of slavery in the South to freedom in the North. Again, Molly practiced giving her Harriet Tubman talk to me. Molly loved her, and told me she was going to get married and name her first child "Harriet."

Molly turned sixteen and shared a big secret with me—she had met a boy she liked! People called him Tiny. Molly couldn't stop talking about him—*Tiny did this, Tiny said that*—and I got tired of hearing about Tiny.

In the growing season I spent a lot of time with Molly because she and I were the main farmers in our families. Mr. Henry made good money hack driving, so he taught Molly and me to do the farming things he usually did. Most important, we learned how to plow with his mule. We worked with the mule, whose name was Sal, plowing the fields to prepare them for the spring planting.

One day, Molly told me that Tiny was coming up to visit. That afternoon, Molly and I were drying dishes in Miz Mildred's kitchen when a horse and wagon pulled up. This tall, nice- looking man jumped out. He was big!

"Where is Tiny?" I asked Molly. She laughed as she ran out of the house towards the wagon and hugged that tall man. I finished drying the dishes and went out to see who was there.

"Willow, meet Tiny Johnson," said Molly. "You are *not* tiny!" I said to the big man.

"I know," he laughed, "but that's what my friends call me."

I decided to call him Big Tiny, but after a while I just called him Tiny, like everyone else.

That spring Molly and Tiny got betrothed. Tiny was learning carpentry as an apprentice. He told us that he and Molly needed to wait several years to get married, so he could get his own carpentry business established. "We want to raise a family," Tiny said, "and I got to be sure I can support them."

I told Tiny, "When you and Molly have a baby girl, you're going to name her Harriet." "You don't say!" said Tiny.

Several years later, one early spring day, Molly and Tiny announced that they would get married in June at their church that was halfway to Birmingham. The wedding party would be in Birmingham because that's where Molly's relatives lived.

That spring was a rough one for my folks because Grampa fell and turned his ankle. He couldn't travel, and Mama had to take care of him. The Henrys invited me to travel with them to the wedding. But I had sworn off ever going back to Birmingham. Every time I thought of Birmingham, I remembered that poor girl with blood oozing down her back.

Miz Mildred knew how I felt because I had shared my secret with her. One day that spring, Miz Mildred sent word through Mama for me to come over to join her for tea. Mama said she thought Mildred was lonely but I figured she wanted to talk to me about the wedding. I was right. Miz Mildred wanted me to go with her and Mr. Henry to Molly's wedding. "You've been Molly's best friend and little sister for your whole life. You've gotta go to her wedding!"

I told Miz Mildred that I couldn't stop thinking about that girl with the bloody back.

"Listen Willow," said Miz Mildred. "There are many Birminghams. Some of those Birminghams are horrible, especially if you are a colored servant at that Fields Plantation. But Molly knows a different Birmingham, with lots of relatives—folks who work hard during the week and cut loose on the weekends.

"You're big enough to travel with me and my husband." Miz Mildred sipped her tea. "Of course, bad things can always happen, but you can't live your life being afraid all the time."

"You mean like my mama?"

"Yes, like your mama," said Mildred. "Your mama has her reasons to be afraid. But if you stay in the house all the time, you miss a lot of fun." I decided to go to Molly's wedding with the Henrys.

We left early in the morning in Mr. Henry's buggy and got to the church in time to change into our Sunday-best clothes. I put on the new dress Mama had sewed for me. Mr. and Mrs. Henry looked very nice in their "parents of the bride" outfits. I brought the blue jay comb that my Chickasaw grandmother had given me, figuring this wedding was a good time to wear it.

Miz Mildred to put it in my hair. Mr. Henry especially liked it. He told me, "My people, the Choctaws, and your people, the Chickasaws, are cousins. They speak the same basic language."

Mr. Henry introduced me to some of his friends, whispering to me that they were part Choctaw, and it was secret. Miz Mildred introduced me to her relatives and her church friends, and they all were nice, making me feel welcome. Some told me that Molly had told them about me. They said they were glad I'd come to the wedding. It was such a beautiful mix of people— all different colors of brown.

The wedding service was beautiful. Everyone knew and loved Molly because she had grown up in this church. Then we traveled to the wedding party in Birmingham. Along the way, I saw lots of people, houses, farms, stores—all very different from the Fields Plantation. We had a good dinner with Tiny's parents and Molly's and Tiny's closest relatives. Mr. Henry introduced me to Tiny's sister. I told her how Molly kept talking about this boy she liked, named Tiny, and I how surprised I was when I met this big guy!

That night was the wedding party at the farm where Miz Mildred's sister lived. It lasted late into the night, and everyone had a good time. I had fun square dancing and flirting with a cute boy. We stayed overnight in the farmhouse, where I shared a bedroom with a bunch of Molly's girl cousins. The next day, I rode with the Henrys all day long back to Pine Hill. I was glad I had gone to Molly's Birmingham.

CHAPTER 16

Women's Circle

I GREW UP ALWAYS BEING the youngest one around. I saw my big brother Thomas get hateful and my best friend Molly get angry. When I finally got to my teen years, I wasn't like either of them. I didn't know what I wanted. I was jealous of Molly because she was so clear that she wanted to get out of Pine Hill. She succeeded in spending most of her time in Birmingham. Then she wanted to get married, and she found a good man and married him.

In June 1879, I finished Pine Hill School. I was twelve years old and had been in school for only four years. But everyone who went to Pine Hill was finished the year they turned twelve. I guess I had learned all that they had to teach me. I could read the newspaper, write sentences, and spell at least some words. I could add and subtract, and knew a little multiplication and division.

Grampa said I was *old enough to keep learning on my own.*

Part of me was glad to be done with school, but most of me was sad because it meant I would no longer see my school friends every day. Sue Ann, Clara Louise, and Peggy Lynn lived quite far from our house. When school ended, I missed them. Sue Ann and I swore that we would remain best friends no matter what. But neither of us was good at writing letters, so it was hard to keep in touch. That summer she sent me an invitation to come to a square dance.

Grampa took me in our buggy, and the square dance was fun. I wrote Sue Ann asking her to meet me at the County Fair, but she couldn't make it. After that, we stopped writing to each other.

I turned thirteen a few months before Molly and Tiny got married. After their honeymoon, Molly came back to stay with her folks to help with the farming. Tiny's carpentry business kept him busy in Birmingham, but every weekend he came up to see his wife. That summer I spent lots of time with Molly, and we had a good time. Molly talked to me about how she had found her path in life as a farmer, a teacher, and a wife. She wanted to be a mother, too. That fall Tiny helped us with the harvest, and afterwards, Molly went back to live all winter in Birmingham with Tiny and his folks.

After Molly got married and left home, I got lonely. In spite of all the places Molly was not allowed to go, she had found her own way. She knew what she wanted and she figured out how to get it.

What was my path in life? After the fall harvest and before the frost, I was hoping to see my Auntie, who really was my Chickasaw grandmother. I wanted to talk to her, but she didn't come to visit that year. Mr. Henry told me he had heard through the grapevine that Auntie's legs couldn't walk all the way down here to see me.

I don't remember much of anything happening that winter. There was constant work to do—taking care of the animals—keeping the wood stocked and the fire going. I got along with Mama and Grampa, but we didn't talk much. Grampa was unsteady on his feet, and walked with a cane. He often took Sugar and the buggy to Pine Hill to tutor children. Mama kept baking up a storm, and Pine Hill Grocery sold everything she made. I told Mama I could help by taking her baked goods to the grocery, so Grampa let me drive Sugar and the buggy to make the deliveries.

Sugar and I became a good team, and I got lots of practice driving that buggy. But Grampa and Mama only let me go to the grocery store. "It ain't proper for a young woman to be out in a buggy by herself," Mama told me.

"Ain't safe," added Grampa.

Mr. and Mrs. Henry went to visit Molly and Tiny in Birmingham, and came back with the news that Molly was expecting a baby. "Just like Molly," I muttered to myself. "She decides she wants to be a mother, and the next thing I know, she's pregnant."

I tried to follow in Molly's footsteps and find my own path. I knew I loved to grow things but wanted to do more than just farming corn, beans, and potatoes. Molly told me growing these crops was *same old—same old*. I wanted to learn how to grow different things, like herbs. I kept thinking about Berta's herb garden in Market Town, where Grampa had taken me years ago when I was small. I wanted to learn from Berta, but I hadn't seen her for a long time. I was restless that winter, as the cold weather dragged on. Grampa was preoccupied with his foot, and Mama was cooking furiously trying to make the tax money.

I talked to Mr. Henry about wanting to work for Berta and asked him if I could get rides with him to Market Town, where he drove his hack almost every day. One day in late winter, Mr. Henry took me to Berta's. It was wonderful to see her again, and we worked together in her garden all day long. We cleared the herb garden of dead leaves and sticks from the winter and planted seeds in her greenhouse.

Miz Berta said she would send word when she needed me to help her again. I waited for several weeks, growing impatient. Maybe I hadn't worked hard enough? Maybe I talked too much?

In early spring, Mildred and Henry went to visit Molly and Tiny. "Molly's getting large with child," Miz Mildred told us when they returned. Then Molly and Tiny came up to visit the Henrys. One morning, I was standing in the cornfield watching a pregnant mama deer with her two yearlings grazing at the edge of the woods. I wondered what it was like to be a mother with another baby on the way. I wondered whether deer helped each other birthing their babies. Then Molly came walking towards me, waving. I ran to see her, noticing her big belly.

She asked, "Do you want to come with me and Mama to Miz Berta's house for dinner tonight? I want to meet Miz Berta because she's a midwife, and soon I'm gonna need her."

"Yes! I want to go with you," I said before Molly finished her sentence. "There's going to be a women's circle at Berta's," Molly added.

"A what?" I'd never heard of a women's circle. Molly told me that it was a group of women who farmed and were interested growing herbs for healing.

"Sounds great!" I replied and went to see Mama in the kitchen.

"I hear there's a meeting for women farmers tonight," Mama said. "Take this cornbread to the meeting. Be sure

to tell Berta how much your Grampa loves her dried nettles—they help his achy joints. Please buy more nettles
from her so I can make him nettle tea every morning."

With a baking pan of cornbread, I traveled up to Market
Town with Molly and her mother. At Berta's house, Molly
and I set the table for six people. I wondered who else
was coming. Soon there was a knock on the door, and
Molly answered it. In came a pretty young woman whose
name was Casey. She had been Berta's assistant for many
years but had recently married and moved to Florence, a
town up on the Tennessee River.

There was another knock, and I ran to open the door.
It was Auntie—my secret grandmother! I helped her with
her bags and cloak. Then we gave each other big hugs. I
was jumping up and down, I was so happy.

"Miz Berta," asked Molly, "How did you get to know
Indian Annie?" I looked up, because I had never heard of
Indian Annie and wondered who they were talking about.

"I've known Indian Annie for many years," replied
Berta, hugging my grandmother. "She knows how to use
herbs for healing. We work together, helping each other."
That's how I learned that my secret grandmother's name
was Indian Annie.

"Berta and I have known each other through good
times and bad," said my grandmother.

We sat down to Miz Berta's yummy dinner. I sat next to
my grandmother—so happy to see her. We kept squeezing
each other's hand under the table. "Can we tell them our
secret?" I whispered to her.

"Yes! These are people we trust," she said. "I will
squeeze your hand to let you know when it is a good
time to tell them."

After we finished eating, we quickly cleared the table and washed the dishes. Then we sat back down at the table, and Miz Berta asked us each to introduce ourselves. The first was Casey, who said that she had learned herbal healing from Miz Berta. She had recently married and moved up to the Tennessee River, and she wanted to use herbs for healing folks up there. Then Miz Mildred and Molly each introduced themselves.

Next came my grandmother, who told everyone her family called her Indian Annie because she was proud of her Chickasaw heritage. But out in public, she said in a quieter tone of voice, she had to pass for white, so we should call her Annie.

Then came me, and Grandmother squeezed my hand, so I announced, "Indian Annie is my real grandmother!"

"Yes," I said to the surprised faces, "I was born an Indian but bad men killed my mother, and my Chickasaw family was starving. So Grandmother found some good white people to take me in. Indian Annie is my grandmother, and she visits me almost every year in the fall and gives me seeds to plant."

I looked up and saw Miz Mildred and Berta hugging each other, and I realized they both knew about me. Molly looked surprised, and so did Casey. Then I added, "I love being Indian, but we have to be quiet and careful. This is our secret, and all of you must keep it secret."

Miz Berta spoke up. "Thank you, Miss Willow, for that beautiful story. We will keep your secret!" Then she smiled, saying "Thank you, Grandmother Indian Annie, for teaching us the herbal healing traditions of your people."

Finally, Miz Berta introduced herself, saying that she was carrying on the herbal medicine traditions of her

Yoruba grandmother, who came over on a slave ship from West Africa. Miz Berta added that she was learning the herbal traditions of this area from Indian Annie.

"Before we get down to business," Berta continued, "we need to be thankful for this wonderful earth that provides us with everything we need with all the plants and all the creatures that are our friends."

We went around the circle again, each of us saying one thing we were thankful for. "This baby getting ready to be born," said Molly.

"My grandchild to be," said Mildred.

"Herbs that survive the winter," said Casey.

"My grandmother," I said.

"My granddaughter," said Indian Annie.

"All of you who are willing to learn from our ancestors," said Miz Berta. I looked around the table at all of us, each with our own different shade of brown.

Then we got down to the business of how to grow more herbs. "Springtime is upon us," said Berta, "Time to plant herbs!"

"We can grow lots of herbs at our farm," offered Miz Mildred, and I nodded in agreement. "We just need to learn how from you experts."

Berta guided us to her greenhouse. "Let's start this year with nettles, because we all can use them, especially us older folks." She gave us some seedlings and lots of seeds. I bought some dried nettles for Grampa.

After the business was finished, we kept chatting. I got to talk to my grandmother and tell her that I had finished school and had time to grow lots of herbs. Grandmother told me she was sorry that she missed coming to see me last fall, but she could no longer walk all that way.

Gus, from her village, had given her a ride to Berta's that day, and she was staying with Berta until Gus came to pick her up.

Berta came over and sat down with me and my grandmother. Indian Annie said, "Willow, I met Berta on the day my daughter—your mother—died. That sad, sad day."

"When I could not save her life," added Berta, wiping her eyes.

Berta and Indian Annie hugged each other. Then Grandmother put her arm around me. "Meeting Berta was the one good thing that came out of that awful day. We have been good friends ever since."

Soon Miz Mildred and Molly announced that they needed to go home. And, of course, that meant I had to go with them. Berta said to me quickly, "Willow, I have springtime work for you, perhaps twice a week. Is that okay with you?"

"Yes! It's a dream come true," I said to Berta, hugging her.

We said our goodbyes, and Molly declared, "We look forward to the next women's circle, the next meeting of Berta's and Indian Annie's School of Herbs!"

That night, as Mr. Henry drove us home my spirits soared. I had grownup friends, part of a women's circle with my favorite people in the world. I was learning not only when to keep secrets, but also when you could share them with people you trust. And Berta had a job for me. I was flying with the wind!

Life was perfect, I thought. But I did not have a crystal ball to see the future.

CHAPTER 17
The Drunk

F OR YEARS, I WORKED FOR Berta two or three days a week. I loved it. Berta taught me the specific needs of each herb and how to care for a garden of herbs and flowers. In the winter, I learned how to manage a greenhouse. In the early spring, our women's circle met and we learned a lot about growing different herbs, especially nettles. During our farm growing season, I worked one or two days a week for Berta and the rest of the days on my family's farm.

Molly gave birth to a healthy baby girl in June 1881. "I'm a proud grandma!" announced Miz Mildred, returning from Birmingham.

"I bet I know your grandbaby's name!" I told Miz Mildred. "Okay, what is it?"

"Harriet!"

"How do you know my granddaughter's name?"

"Molly taught me about Harriet Tubman, and she told me Harriet would be the name of her first girl child." I replied.

"Sounds like Molly!" laughed Miz Mildred.

After Harriet's birth, Molly and Tiny spent most of their time in Birmingham and just came up for short visits. Grampa and I decided to plant a smaller cornfield.

The Henrys had a growing family, so they increased the size of their cornfield. Their nephews, Simon and Daniel, moved up here to help with the farming. I kept working for Berta at least one day a week.

That winter, the Henrys wanted to spend time with their grandchild. Molly needed their help because Tiny's carpentry business was booming, and he had to travel to some of his jobs. So the Henrys went to Birmingham, and I took care of their livestock as well as ours, milking two cows every morning. And I also traveled to Market Town several days a week to work for Berta in her greenhouse. Life was good. I was happy.

The spring I turned fifteen, Berta asked me to stay for a week in Market Town, because she had three expectant mothers. "One never knows exactly when those babies will come, and I am only one person," Berta explained. "I need you to care for my greenhouse, which is full of seedlings, and to weed the garden." Fortunately, I could agree to take the job because the Henrys were back home, and they could milk my family's cows, as well as theirs. Simon and Daniel would take care of our fields. That Monday morning, Mr. Henry gave me a ride in his buggy up to Market Town.

Berta explained to her long-time boarders—Esther, Louise, and Betsy—that I would be staying the week. Esther showed me around the upstairs of the house, including the empty bedroom where I would sleep. It was a nice little room with a small bed, a dresser, and a window looking onto the street.

Through the window, I could see a beautiful catalpa tree with a huge trunk and big leaves. Looking closer, I saw beautiful, tiny flowers blooming in the wide leaves.

That night Berta, Esther, Louise, Betsy, and I sat out on Berta's front porch, admiring the blooming catalpa.

The next day, town workers came and cut down our catalpa tree. They said they were widening the street. They sawed up all the branches, leaving just an ugly stump.

"No respect for the beauty of a living tree," complained Berta.

"They told us they were making the street wider," said Louise. "But how'd we know they meant to make it ugly?"

"They can keep their dang street," muttered Esther. "I want our catalpa tree back!"

Several days went by and, in spite of the poor catalpa tree's demise, I was enjoying myself. I got to know Esther, Louise, and Betsy. They were all middle-aged colored women, and they insisted I call them by their first names with no *Miss* or *Miz* attached. "Otherwise, we're gonna feel like old maids!" laughed Louise.

They pampered me. Esther braided my hair. When it was chilly or rainy in the evenings, we played cards at the kitchen table. When the weather was nice, we sat on the front porch after supper. Porch sitting, they called it. Their neighbors would stop by to chat and tell jokes.

After the neighbors left, Esther, Louise and Betsy filled me in on all the latest gossip. Living in Market Town was very different from living way out in the country.

One morning, Berta asked me to bring tea to the greenhouse so we could talk. I expected she would tell me her latest ideas about how to raise herbs. Instead she brought up something I'd never thought about.

"Willow," Berta said, "I had an unusual guest yesterday. He is a man I talked to only once, over a decade ago."

Then Berta frowned, and paused for a long time. I sipped my tea, looked around the greenhouse, and waited.

Finally, Berta looked at me intently, "His name is Joe Finley. I met him the night your mother died." Berta paused, "He loved your mother ..."

"Oh, that's nice to know," I chatted. "I guess a lot of people loved her. My grandmother always said she was like a ray of morning sunshine, and ..."

"Willow, listen." Berta shook her head, trying to pry words out of her mouth. "He's your father," she whispered.

"My father?" No one had ever told me about a father. "Did my father kill my mother?"

"No! Oh no! It was the Ku Klux Klan that killed your mother," exclaimed Berta. "Those KKKs can't stand the idea of white and colored people loving each other. Joe Finley loved your mother, but his father was in the Ku Klux Klan. The KKK attacked—and killed—your mother because she was Indian. Joe's father sent Joe on an errand so he would be away when they attacked your mother."

My stomach tightened as Berta spoke. I felt far away, wanted all this to stop. But Berta kept talking.

"Joe Finley didn't know anything about the attack until hours later." Berta went on. "He went to the Sheriff and found out that I was nursing your mother, trying to save her life. Late that night, Joe came over here to my house. He was distraught, so angry at his father. He and I talked. He told me he hated his father and couldn't stand to be around him. That night your mother died. The next morning Joe left home to go out west somewhere. He's been out there all these years."

Berta frowned and shook her head. "Joe's father died a month ago, so Joe came back here. He wants to see you."

I sat there, trying to follow what Berta was saying. It was the first I had heard anyone say anything about me having a father. My head hurt. I didn't know what to think.

Berta had to leave to go see her expectant mothers. I sat there alone in her greenhouse. Finally, I got up and did some chores. That night I wasn't hungry and didn't join the porch sitters. I went to my room and lay down there for a long time in the darkness until I fell asleep. The next morning, I woke up wondering about my father. When Berta and I were alone, I asked her what my father was like.

"I don't know him well, but he seems like a good man," she said. "I do believe he loved your mother and he loved you. He told me that when your mother and her brothers came down to Market Town to sell their crops, Spring would carry you in a sling on her back. Joe loved seeing you, and playing with you."

That day I raked Berta's yard. In the afternoon, I saw a man standing on the sidewalk in front of Berta's house. He was looking at me while I worked. He was a white man with dark eyes and dark hair, dressed like they do in Texas, with a cowboy hat and boots. He looked at me with sad eyes, and for a moment our eyes met. Then I looked away, and he turned and slowly walked away.

That evening I told Berta I saw a man looking at me, a man wearing a cowboy hat and boots.

"That's him," said Berta. "He wants to meet you. It is entirely up to you. If you want to meet him, I can be there with you." I thought about it. I was curious. He looked like he might be nice. I liked his cowboy boots.

At nine the next morning, Berta and I sat on the front porch, and the mysterious Texan came up to the gate. Berta asked him to join us.

"Mr. Joe Finley," Berta said, "this is Willow."

"Howdy-do?" asked the man.

"I'm fine," I replied. And then we ran out of things to say.

The man wiped a spot off his cowboy boots. He cleared his throat, hemmed, and hawed. Finally, Joe Finley said, "Miss Willow, I'm so sad about what happened to your mother. I loved your mother, and I loved holding you when you were a baby."

Then he paused. "I hate what my father did. I hate him. I left this town and never spoke to him again," Joe Finley said, then buried his head in his arms and wept.

After a time, he said, "I'm glad my father is finally dead, and I'm sure as shootin' that he's in the meanest streets of hell." Then he took out a handkerchief, and wiped his eyes.

I didn't know what to say. "Are you all right?" Miz Berta asked to me. I didn't answer. Then she said to Joe, "I think that's enough for today."

The next day, one of Berta's expectant mothers went into labor with her first child. George, her neighbor and business partner, was her driver when she needed to go out of town. He drove Berta out to the countryside, and no one knew how long Berta would be away. Births can go quickly or take a very long time. I put in a long work-day in the garden, and I was tired. I ate supper in the kitchen with Esther and Louise and then went to bed. Sleep came quickly.

Suddenly someone was pounding on my bedroom door. I woke up. It was the dead of night. The knocking got louder and louder. "Willow, open up the door," a voice said, "it's your father. Open up the door!"

The man who said he was my father sounded funny, slurring his words. He sounded like the drunk who hung around the Pine Hill Grocery begging for money. Mama always told me, "That man's drunk. Stay away from him." And I did.

I had just met my father the day before. And now he sounded like a drunk, calling my name, "*Willow, Willow, open up this door–I'm your father. Please—I love you, I need to talk to you.*"

I had latched my bedroom door the way Berta had showed me, pushing the piece of wood nailed to the doorframe so that it stopped the door from opening. I tried to ignore the voice calling my name. Suddenly the wooden latch, nail and all, flew across my room! The bedroom door swung open, and my father staggered into my room. I sat up in bed, pulling the covers up over my knees and shoulders. The man crossed the room, grabbed my arms and lifted me out of the bed. The stink of alcohol engulfed him.

"Spring!" he mumbled, "I love you, Spring." Spring? That was my mother's name!

"I am not *Spring!*" I shouted. "Let me go! Leave me alone!"

"Oh, Spring—Spring, my love!" he kept saying, putting his arms around me, putting his hands on my body.

"Stop!" I yelled, trying to get away from him. But he was stronger than me. He put his arms around me even tighter, kissing my shoulders."

"STOP!" I yelled as loud as I could, kicking him, but it was like kicking a freight train.

Suddenly someone yelled, "Get your hands off that child!" It was Berta coming though the bedroom door, pointing her long-handled pistol at the drunken man holding me. Suddenly he let go and kneeled down on the floor. Facing Berta, he raised his hands above his head in surrender.

I heard noise behind Berta, someone running up the stairs. George appeared with a coil of rope. While Berta kept her gun pointed at my father, George quickly tied his hands behind his back and forced him to sit in a chair. Then George tied his legs and waist tightly to the chair. After the man was tied up, George sat on my bed and pulled out his pistol, guarding the tied-up drunk who said he was my father.

Berta put her gun in her holster, came to me, and put a blanket over my shoulders. She was still wearing her coat and hat. She and George must have just gotten home. Berta led me downstairs to the kitchen, where her three women boarders were huddled around the table. I was shaking like a leaf, despite the warm blanket. While Berta took off her coat, Esther sat me down on a kitchen chair and put her arm around me.

Berta looked at us sitting there and said, "Esther, you look like you could be Willow's mother. Your skin and hair are the same color." Then Berta said, "I have a plan. I'll be back down here soon to talk to you all." Berta left me with her boarders and went back upstairs where George still guarded the drunk. We sat silently in Berta's kitchen.

At that moment it was comforting to be held by someone who looked like she could be my mother. Meanwhile, Louise fired up the kitchen woodstove and heated up water for tea. She put some leftover biscuits on a plate. The tea and biscuits helped me stop shaking. I put my head down in Esther's lap, feeling suddenly very tired. But I couldn't sleep, I felt numb and far away. All I could do was stare under the kitchen table, at the bathrobed legs of Berta's boarders. They chatted, their voices sounding far away.

Berta stayed upstairs for a long time. I wondered what would happen next. I started shivering again. Fear gripped me.

After a long time, Berta came back into the kitchen. The man and woman who lived nearby came into the kitchen with Berta. "Mr. and Mrs. Whitley are going to the sheriff's office to report that a drunk man broke into this house and disturbed the peace," Berta said. "They will ask the sheriff to take that drunk away from here to the jail." The Whitleys quickly left for the sheriff's office.

I sat up, and looked at Berta.

"Willow, I'm glad you're awake," she said. "Did your father hurt you?"

I could no longer think of that man as my father. "He is not my father!" I said. "I hate him. I want him sent to prison."

"Tell me what he did to you," Berta asked.

"He grabbed me, he kissed me, he touched me!" I said in a rush of words.

"Did he force his manhood on you?"

I thought for a moment. I had never heard those words, *force his manhood*. But I realized I knew what it meant. I had watched the big bull mate with our milk cow.

"That man did not force his manhood on me," I said quietly, unconsciously imitating Berta's deep southern accent, not quite accepting those words as my own. "But he did hurt my arms." I pulled my arms out from under the cover, and pointed to where he had grabbed me and pulled me out of bed.

Berta looked at both my arms, which still ached from that man grabbing me. "You're a tough farm girl," said Berta gently. "You don't bruise easily. Thank goodness you are okay."

"Thank goodness you got home when you did," I said to Berta. But Berta wasn't listening, she was talking.

"Everyone, listen carefully. Our first goal is to get the drunk out of our house. Our second goal is to keep quiet about what happened to Willow."

Berta paused, then looked at me, speaking in a low, intense voice: "Joe is a white man and we are a colored household. That means *no crime has been committed*, according to the laws of Alabama."

"But Joe *should* be punished!" I whispered, my voice shaking.

She looked me, her expression serious, no longer gentle. "Willow," she said. "When you are at your grandfather and Mama's house, you are considered white. But when you are here, *you are colored!*"

Berta sat down across from me and took my hands in hers. "Willow, if you try to punish Joe for what he did to you, it will blow up in your face. And it will destroy the lives of *all* of us who live in this house, including you.

"We must keep this out of the courts and out of the newspapers." Berta added, "And especially out of the gossip network."

I tried to look away, but Berta firmly held my hands until I met her gaze. "Willow," she said, "No matter how truthful you are in describing what happened to you— the sheriff, the newspaper, the politicians, will turn what happened upside down into something we colored people brought upon ourselves."

Berta looked straight into my eyes. "Joe *should* be punished," she continued, "But that won't happen, no matter what we do. If a Negro man had done the same thing that Joe did to you, there would be a lynch mob out there right now, determined to kill that black man."

Tears ran down my face. "That man is *not* my father! I hate him!"

Berta put her hand gently on my shoulder. "We will talk more later," she said. "Right now, we got to get that drunk out of this house." Berta left us to go back up the stairs. Louise and Betsy followed Berta, and went into their rooms to try to sleep. Esther stayed with me. We tried to sleep there at the kitchen table. I put my head back in Esther's lap. Esther put her head on the table and dozed fitfully. I couldn't sleep, aware of every little sound.

Hours later, the harsh light of the sheriff's lantern suddenly shone on us. Esther woke up, and we both sat up. The sheriff questioned Esther about who she was and who I was. Esther told the sheriff that I was her niece, that I lived with her family way out in the countryside. She made it all sound true. Then Esther added that I was working for Berta, and the drunk man broke into the house and into my room—that he grabbed me but had not hurt me.

Then the sheriff asked me. "Is this true?"

I nodded, and whispered, "Yes." Just as Berta had told me.

The sheriff nodded at me, and then said to Berta, "We're going to take Joe Finley to the jail and dry him out. He will be in jail only a day or two. During that time, Berta, you need to put good metal locks on the front and back doors of your house. And you need to put metal bar locks inside all the bedroom doors."

Berta nodded yes.

Then the sheriff went upstairs. From the kitchen we heard the drunk stumbling down the stairs. Then the sheriff and his deputy hauled him out the front door and off to jail. Esther took me upstairs to her room, and I crawled into bed with her and fell asleep.

It took me a long time to get over my drunk father attacking me. I never saw him again, but months later I did receive a letter from him. He sent it to Berta, asking her to give it to me. This is what he wrote:

Dear Willow,

I am sorry for what I did. I want to tell you my story. Maybe you will forgive me. Your mother Spring was my love—we were as man and wife. We had a baby named Willow, and we loved her. Then my father killed Spring—he wrecked my life! A year ago my father died, and I came back to Alabama to see my brothers, aunts, and uncles.

I wanted to see you. In my mind's eye, you were still a little girl. I did not realize you were already a young woman. Then I saw you—and you looked just like Spring! You moved like Spring. It was like a dream come true. I watched you. I wanted to be near you. I needed you.

I drank way too much whiskey. I lost my head.

I don't remember much about that night. I woke up in jail. I am sorry for what I did or said. I don't remember any of it.

Now I am back in Texas. My buddies and I signed up to repair the railroad tracks that run all the way to California. We leave tomorrow.

I apologize for whatever I did or said. I am mailing this to Berta because I know her address. I will not bother you again. Never, ever. I am done with Alabama.

Sincerely, Joe Finley

Months later, I decided I was glad he sent me that letter. It made me understand him a little better. But I never, ever wanted to see him again.

CHAPTER 18

Hidden Village

THE MORNING AFTER MY DRUNK father attacked me, I woke up in a strange bed. It was Esther's bed, and I saw Esther slipping quietly out her door. Dread crept over me as I remembered the night before— that man kissing me, his hands feeling my body. He *said* he was my father, but he called me *Spring. He acted like I was his wife!*

I never knew my mother or my father. But I hated that disgusting man who called himself my father. I felt dizzy, confused. I closed my eyes, curled up in a ball, and tried to go back to sleep. But the memories kept coming: Berta saving me with her gun, George tying him up, the sheriff asking Esther questions, Berta explaining that *no crime had been committed* because that drunk was white, and I was colored. I wanted it all to disappear.

The world had suddenly become dark. Sunlight shone through the window, but how could it be a sunny day after such a terrible night? I looked out the window and saw that ugly stump that used to be a beautiful catalpa tree. I felt like that stump.

"How dare my own father do that to me!" I muttered under my breath. Anger coursed through me. What he did sure felt like a crime to me. "He's *not* my father," I swore to myself.

Suddenly, I sat up. Today I was supposed to go home—back to Mama and Grampa. "No!" I said out loud to no one. I couldn't go back to Mama and Grampa. What would I say? How could I explain what had happened to me?

I looked around Esther's room. Esther had neatly folded my clothes and put them on her chair. I dressed quickly and headed for the kitchen. Berta met me on the stairs, "How are you, dear?" she asked me.

"Uh...not good," I mumbled.

"Esther's fixed some breakfast for you," Berta said as she went by me. "I'll be back down to the kitchen shortly."

Esther fed me a scrambled egg and cornbread. I tried to eat, but felt sick to my stomach. I thanked her for letting me sleep in her bed. "We have to take care of each other," she said.

As I finished eating, Berta entered the kitchen. I said to her, "Thank you Berta, for saving me last night."

"You are welcome," Berta replied. "Do you remember that you are supposed to go home to your mama today?"

"I don't want to go home today. I don't know what to say. I'm afraid."

"Yes, fear can linger," said Berta, and she thought for a while before saying, "You could come with me up to Indian Annie's village. I need to go up there to check on Annie and pick up some dried herbs that they grew last summer. Do you want to go with me?"

"Yes," I whispered. "Yes, I've never been up to my grandmother's village. Been wanting to go for a long time."

But Mama and Grampa expected me to come home that day. Berta must have read my mind. "Write a note to your folks, and I'll get George to deliver it to them." I wrote a note explaining that Berta needed me to help her that day, and that I'd be home by the following night.

"It will be good to go up to Annie's village," said Berta.

Berta and I packed our overnight bags, and I put them in her buggy. George hitched up Berta's horse, Treasure. Berta gave me the reins to drive Treasure while we traveled North on the Military Road. We went through a broad valley with mountains on both sides of us, passing farms large and small. The further north we traveled— the fewer the farms and the fewer the travelers on the road. I loved driving Berta's horse and buggy.

Gradually, the mountains got closer, the woods got thicker, and the road got rougher. There were sections of roadway that had been flooded out. Berta told me that we were approaching a place to rest, and she directed me where to pull off the road. We got out, stretched our legs, and relieved ourselves. We gave Treasure water and let her graze while we drank the clear spring water coming out of the hillside and ate Esther's cornbread.

Then Berta took the reins, and we continued on the Military Road. After a while, Berta turned off the road, and we got out. We walked up a narrow trail leading westward, Berta leading the way and me following her, leading Treasure and the buggy. We came into a small village about the size of Pine Hill. There was a schoolhouse, a general store, a blacksmith shop, a church, and some houses.

"This village is called Two Trails Crossing," Berta told me. She stopped in front of the church and knocked on the door of a small house. A man opened the door.

"Good afternoon, Preacher Jones!" said Berta, shaking the man's hand. "I've come to see Annie, and wondered if I could leave my buggy with you? I'll take my horse with me."

"Sure thing." said the preacher to Berta. Then Berta introduced me as her assistant. "Good to meet you," said Preacher Jones to me. We unhitched Treasure and pulled the buggy into the stable.

After saying thank you and goodbye, Berta and I headed up a narrow trail on foot. I led Treasure, paying attention to both her footing and mine. "This was just a narrow foot trail until a few years ago, when folks tried to make it a horse trail," Berta explained. "But the spring rain washed part of it out. Mother Earth is trying to reclaim it."

We walked for what felt like a long time. The sun was getting low, and we quickened our pace, not wanting to be caught on this rough terrain in the dark. We turned a sharp corner around a rocky outcrop, and suddenly there was a big barn right in front of us.

"Yoo-hoo!" called Berta.

A young man appeared. "Miss Berta—hello!" he called, running up and shaking her hand. "Gus," Berta said, "this is Willow."

I was surprised. Here was a second white man who knew Berta by name. Gus led Treasure into the barn, and Berta and I followed him. Then Berta opened a door in the back of the barn, and I followed her through that door into a yard with a farmhouse across the way.

"How do these white men know you?" I asked Berta.

"If you help people when they are sick and you deliver their babies, people remember you." said Berta.

We walked up the steps to the farm house, and an older white woman opened the door, hugged Berta, and then invited us in.

"Nellie Jean, meet Spring's daughter, Willow," said Berta. I was shocked. Berta was *telling my secret* to a stranger!

"Mercy me!" exclaimed the older white woman, wrapping her arms around me. "Willow, this is Gus' mother," Berta told me.

Berta kept talking, explaining that we wanted to visit Annie. Nellie Jean said it was too late to go up to Annie's village today. The sun was going down, and soon it would be dark.

"Gus," the woman called to the young man. "Show Willow around the farm, while Berta and I catch up."

It didn't take Gus long to show me the cows, horses, pigs, chickens, cornfield, vegetable garden, and pasture. I told him I lived on a farm.

I was more interested in asking him questions about things that didn't make sense to me. Why did he and the older woman know my secrets? Why was his family's barn blocking the trail?

"Do you know Grandmother Annie?" I asked Gus, as we walked back towards the house. "Yes," he said. "We call her Indian Annie around here."

"Don't you have to keep her secret?"

"We have to keep the *whole village's* secret." Gus responded. "But it's not near as hard as it used to be during the war. Now all our kids go to the new public school in Two Trails Crossing."

"Do you know who I am?" I asked Gus. with a look I learned from my school teacher when asking me a hard question, a look that look meant "don't be shy."

"Yes, you are Indian Annie's granddaughter. Your mother, Spring, was killed by the Ku Klux Klan when you were a baby. I was a little kid then. I am very sorry about your mom."

I wasn't thinking about my mom right then. "Were you living up here when my mother was killed?"

"Yes. Me and my ma and pa were living here. You see, the Confederate army forced my father to be a soldier. He ran away from the army during the war. I was just a little kid, and my ma, pa, and I were running and hiding. We were starving, and the Indians in this village saved us. After the war, we built this farm so enemies couldn't ride up the trail right into the hidden village."

"Is that why the barn blocks the trail?"

"Yes," said Gus.

We walked back to the farmhouse, and my mind was whirling, trying to piece together what Gus had told me.

When we got back in the farm house, Gus told his mother and Berta that I had "grilled" him. And they all laughed.

"Willow and Berta, why don't you settle into our guestroom, so I can get to cooking and you can rest after your long trip," said Nellie Jean.

Berta and I went upstairs to the guest room, where Berta always stayed when she visited here. I lay down and must have dozed, because when I woke up Berta was not there. It was dark outside, and soon I heard a bell ring for dinner. The food was good, and I met Gus' father and younger sister. That night, as I crawled into bed, I realized I had forgotten about that drunk for much of the day. Instead, I was learning secrets about my life, secrets that made me happy.

In the morning, after breakfast Berta and I walked up to the hidden village. The trail started right behind the Logan's farmhouse, which had been positioned to protect Indian Annie's village. I didn't even see the trail until we were on it. It wound through the woods, then along a narrow rocky ledge. Suddenly, the trail ended in a beautiful meadow with a mountain ridge on the far side. I could see a stream running through the meadow, and there were seven or eight small log homes. Beyond the meadow, I saw vegetable gardens and cornfields.

"I need to go alone to care for Indian Annie," Berta told me. "She's too sick to see anyone but me."

I stopped walking, and watched Berta crossing the meadow. A girl ran out of another log cabin, close to where I stood. She was about my size, and followed by a bunch of small children. "Hi Willow," said the girl. "I'm Misty, your cousin." It was so strange to be in a place where people I had never seen knew my name!

"How did you know Berta and I were here?" I asked Misty.

"Yesterday when you arrived, Gus whistled from his house. We have a code, and his whistle meant—*friends are here*. Then last night, he walked up here to tell us it was you and Berta. Annie has been very sick, and we are very glad Berta has come to help us take care of her. And it is wonderful to see you, our long-lost Willow."

Misty fetched her moccasins, and asked the two children if they wanted to come with us to help show me around their village. The children told me the names of the people who lived in each little log house. Misty told me how each person who lived there was related to me—everyone was an aunt, uncle or cousin. Then the two children left us to play with their cousins.

"Is my mother Spring buried here?" I asked Misty, as we continued our tour of the village.

"Yes, do you want to see her grave?" said Misty, and I followed her all the way behind the cornfields to their graveyard, near where the rocky ridge rose up out of the ground. The graves where the relatives were buried were marked by rocks, logs, or by trees. Misty showed me my mother's grave, which was marked by a smooth, round rock. I knelt on the ground, and as I touched that rock, my heart pounded. Misty showed me the graves of other relatives. She told me the names of each person buried there.

"Do you want to go to Indian Annie's house?" Misty asked me. "Since she got sick, Annie has been staying next door at her sister Eve's house. But I can show you Annie's empty house, where your mother Spring used to live. It's where you were born."

We walked over to the little log house, and Misty opened the heavy wood door. Inside was one room with no windows, and it took a few moments for my eyes to adjust to the darkness. I sat in a straight-back chair and looked at the fireplace that took up much of one wall of the room. A table, two chairs, and two narrow beds filled the room. Articles of clothing hung from a row of pegs on the back wall. Everything was tidy and well-swept by a broom that rested next to the door.

I sat there, imagining living in this house with Annie. This was where I was born and where my mother nursed me. I tried to imagine my mother. I started to doze off, but someone knocked at the door and woke me up. Berta entered and introduced me to Eve, my grandmother's sister.

"Annie sends her love," said Eve, taking my hand. "You look so much like your mother. Please come visit us again soon, any time."

Berta told me that we needed to leave to get back on the Military Road before it got dark. We walked back to the Logan farm, and Gus walked with us, leading Treasure, to Two Trails Crossing. There he hitched up Treasure to the buggy and led her all the way to the Military Road, as Berta and I followed. When we got to the Military Road, we thanked Gus, and got on the road heading south.

CHAPTER 19

Path in Life

"**G**US IS A NICE YOUNG man." said Berta, as Treasure pulled our buggy southward.

"I was just thinking that," I said. "Not like that terrible man who said he was my father."

"Now is a good time for us to talk," said Berta. And she handed me the reins. "You drive, I'll talk," she said.

"Being attacked like you were is a terrible thing," Berta started. "Many young girls have been hurt far worse than you were. It is especially bad on those plantations where the rich white men can do whatever they want—murder, rape, torture. And they get away with it. They *never* get punished!"

I was glad we were the only people on the road. "Did this ever happen to you?" I asked Berta as Treasure clip-clopped along.

"Yes, child, it did. It is very hard to talk about." I watched Berta thinking, shaking her head. "It's hard, but I'm going to tell you. It will be another of our secrets."

I nodded and whispered, "Cross my heart and hope to die."

"I was born on the Barton Plantation in southern Alabama," Berta said. "Both my parents were slaves on that plantation. My mother worked in the house, my father in the field. The plantation was owned by James Barton, who was crippled when his wagon fell on him. I was a baby at that time. Mr. Barton was a kind man to me and Mama, and so was his wife, Miz Abigail. Their oldest son, James, Jr. was a horrible, *horrible* man. He was arrogant, mean, and very happy that his father was crippled, and could no longer run the plantation.

"Mr. and Mrs. Barton were elderly, and they decided to give their plantation to their son and move up to the hills, where it was cooler in the summer. They bought a house in Market Town, the house I live in.

"My mother cared for Mr. Barton after his accident," Berta continued. "The Bartons brought my mama with them to Market Town to take care of them in their old age. I was just a small girl at that time, and so I came with my mother."

Berta took out a handkerchief, and wiped her eyes.

"Just before we left that plantation, their son Junior, had his way with me. He was in his twenties, and strong. He sent me to get something from his bedroom, and then he followed me into his room and locked the door behind him. He gagged me with a rag. He raped me. I kicked and tried to scream, to no avail.

"That is my story. I was only ten years old. It's not at all unusual on a plantation. Those rich white men can do whatever they want. Mr. and Mrs. Barton never found out."

We rode for a while in silence. Then I asked, "What happened next?"

"A few days after I got raped, I moved with my mother to Mr. and Mrs. Barton's new house in Market Town," said Berta. "Mama and I took care of Master James Barton and Miz Abigail.

They brought one other slave with them. George was a kid in his teens and was good with horses. His father had been Mr. and Mrs. Barton's driver, and George followed in his father's footsteps.

"Miz Abigail Barton died during the Civil War. After the war ended, George and I were no longer slaves. Mr. Barton deeded his house and the four acres around it to George and me. After Mr. Barton died, George and I inherited the house and the land. We divided the land, me taking the house, and George taking three of the four acres. George built himself a house right next door to mine and married a colored lady. They have been my neighbors ever since. George built a stable and a pasture to keep his horses and set up a hack business to taxi people around Market Town. We are still neighbors, best friends, and business associates. Because we were colored people who owned two houses next door to each other, our street became a mixed neighborhood—colored people and immigrants, Italians and Jews. And we get along just fine with our neighbors.

"Did you ever marry?"

"No, sweet child, I didn't. I think that rape ruined me as far as getting married. Or maybe it's the way I am by nature. I just wanted to be an old maid. When I was young and pretty, many a colored man tried to court me, but I just wasn't interested. Lucky for me, I was an independent woman with a successful boarding house and midwifery business."

We rode on in silence. After a long while, Berta told me, "We're going all the way to Pine Hill to your Grampa's house. I want to be sure to get you home tonight."

I realized I was running out of time to ask Berta questions. "How do I ... How did you ... get over that bad man?" I asked her.

"Bad things happen to many people," Berta said. "Mostly, you just have to pick yourself up and do what you can with what you got."

"Do you think Joe really is my father?" "Yes, I *know* he is your father."

Treasure slowed down, and I got out and gave her water. Berta took the reins as we got back on the road.

"I knew Joe's mom," Berta said. "I helped birth her sons, including Joe. Joe's mom was the strong one in that family. When she died, her husband fell apart and took to drink. After the war ended, Joe's dad and his buddies joined the Ku Klux Klan.

"The night after Spring was attacked and raped, Joe came to my house," Berta continued. "He was so angry at his father. And there is no doubt in my mind that he truly loved Spring, your mother. And he loved their baby, which was you."

"The day after Spring died, Joe left town. He went out west where lots of sad, angry people go to escape whatever makes them sad and angry. Like many others, Joe drank to ease his pain." Berta paused, "Your Mama Rose gave you good advice about drunks—stay away from them."

I started thinking about all that. But we were near my home, and I still had another question. "Berta, how do you find your path in life?" I asked.

"You make your path by walking," she replied.

"I know. But how did you know that you wanted to be a healer?"

"I followed in my mother's footsteps. I took care of people. She had learned about herbal medicines from her mother, who learned it from her Yoruba people across the ocean. My mama taught me. As a teenager, I made friends with a midwife and I tagged along with her, assisting her for many years. I also learned how to run a house. I had to figure out how to make money to pay the bills and the taxes, so I made it a boarding house. As far as herbs, I was always interested in plants, so I learned about herb farming by growing herbs."

We approached my house. But I had more to say. "I don't know how to find my path in life," I said. "I can't follow in Mama Rose's footsteps, because I'm so different from her. And I never knew my birth mother."

"Don't wallow in self-pity, Willow." Berta said quickly. "You have a good home and family. You are clearly a gifted farmer. I think you're already finding your path in life."

The next morning, I had to get back to hoeing because the weeds were swallowing up our corn. I was the only one working in the fields. I had a lot to think about, and was glad to be alone.

That fall, a man from the Market Town Court House came to take a photograph of Grampa because Grampa had been a county judge. They wanted his photograph for the new courthouse. I was working in the cornfield near the house. I saw the man arrive in his buggy and watched him go into the house. A little while later, Grampa and the man came out together. I was far away from them and couldn't hear their conversation. I figured Grampa was telling him about our farm. Then Grampa called to me, "Willow, stand still right there in front of the corn."

I didn't know why Grampa said that, but I did what he said. I put the hoe down and just stood there, thinking my own thoughts. Then the man left in his buggy, and I went back to hoeing.

A few weeks later, Grampa got a package in the mail. There were two carefully-wrapped photographs in it. One was Grampa, looking elegant in his top hat and best suit. The other photo, to my surprise, was me standing in the corn field! I didn't know that man took a photograph of me. I thought he was just talking to Grampa. These were the first photographs our family ever had. Grampa framed both of them and set them on the mantlepiece over our fireplace in the living room. At the time, I hated that picture of me. I thought it made me look ugly and dirty. But as the years went by, I changed my mind. I saw in that photograph all the confusing thoughts and feelings going on in my life at that moment.

CHAPTER 20

Bethrothed

"SIXTEEN IS MARRYING AGE FOR girls," Mama told me on my sixteenth birthday. "You need to get out of the house and go to church socials so you can meet decent young men." I took my mama's advice and went to one church social. I hated it. Bull's younger brothers were there, the boys who had knocked me down when I was little. They were still showing off, and the girls were flirting back—batting their eyelashes and giggling at them.

"Let me out of here." I said to myself. "I don't need socials. I don't want to meet boys."

I was plenty busy. We were short-staffed on our farm. Grampa's bad foot prevented him from working in the fields. Molly was living in Birmingham with her husband and baby daughter. Mr. Henry was hack-driving in Market Town. Miz Mildred was getting on in age and complaining that her old bones meant she couldn't do field work anymore. She cooked with Mama, and they made good money because their pies and cornbread always sold out at the Pine Hill Grocery. How were we going to keep the farm going, if it was only me working full-time in the field?

The Henrys solved the problem by taking in their nephews Simon and Daniel to live with them and work the fields. Me and those two boys were responsible for keeping our two farms weeded between the planting and the harvesting. I taught them what I knew, and we often worked together.

I continued to work part-time for Berta. The fear of my drunken father faded over time, but I never again stayed overnight at Berta's. I always traveled back and forth to Market Town with Mr. Henry. I went there when Mr. Henry went, and came home when he came home. He and I were good friends. He told me stories about the Choctaws, and I told him about Grandmother Annie's hidden village.

I learned a lot from Berta. I managed her greenhouse in the winter and kept her herb garden in the summer. I kept my own schedule, working three days a week in the cold weather and one day a week in the summer. I especially loved working in her greenhouse in the winter, feeling the warmth of the sun through the glass ceiling. I planted, harvested, dried, sorted, bagged, and labeled various medicinal herbs for Berta's healing practice.

Sometimes it was dark when Mr. Henry and I rode home. Right before we crossed the bridge over the Abookoshi River, we passed a big old rundown house with peeling paint and junk around the yard. When it was dark, I would often see young girls standing outside that house, next to the road. They had on highfalutin' women's clothes, big fur coats, and fancy shoes.

I asked Mr. Henry about them. He said, "Nothing of concern to you."

But I kept asking him questions about those girls. Ordinarily soft-spoken, Mr. Henry raised his voice,

"Willow, count your blessings. Those girls are out there so they can eat."

"But they have fancy clothes on!" I cried.

"They sell themselves to whoever pays them," said Mr. Henry, exasperated. "There but for fortune go you or I."

He drove on, and I started to ask him …

"No more questions," Mr. Henry barked at me. "I will *not* say any more about it. And you won't either if you want to get rides from me."

I stopped asking Mr. Henry questions. But those girls troubled my sleep. One night, I dreamed I was standing out there with them, shivering in the cold. A man rode up in a buggy and told me to get in. It was that drunk who said he was my father. I said, "No—go away!" He grabbed my arm, pulling me. And I woke up in a sweat, my heart pounding.

When I turned seventeen, Mama pestered me about going to socials. "Otherwise," she said, "you're likely to end up an old maid."

I remembered Berta telling me that she *wanted* to be an old maid. Berta was not interested in men. I decided that being an old maid like Berta was fine with me. Mama disagreed, "Becoming an old maid is the *worst thing* that can happen to a pretty young girl."

I paid Mama no mind, and turned eighteen, nineteen— and then twenty. "You're wasting your life," said Mama.

But I had good friends and good work, and that's all I wanted. There were Berta and Esther in Market Town, Mr. and Mrs. Henry, and of course Mama and Grampa. And Molly—when she visited her folks. Sometimes I saw my school friends Sue Ann, Clara Louise, and Peggy Lynn. One year we went to the County Fair together, and they invited me to go square dancing with them. We had fun that year. But by the next year, they all had boyfriends. They wanted to *fix me up* with a boy. But I wasn't interested. Then they all got married and stopped inviting me to things.

I was twenty-one and well on my way to becoming an old maid. One day, Grampa brought a young man home with him for dinner. His name was William Brown. Grampa had met him at an education meeting in Market Town. William worked in Birmingham at the Public Education Office, and he was traveling to rural public schools around Alabama.

At dinner, he told us he was trying to strengthen the teaching of children's literature and improve the relationship between public schools and libraries.

"We need better public libraries," he added. I agreed with him.

William was good-looking and smart. He was a tall, trim white man with brown hair and grey eyes. I was drawn to him like a moth to fire. When he came around, my heart tingled and my head got fuzzy.

"Grampa knows how to pick 'em," Mama whispered to me, reminding me that Grampa brought a young Thomas Fields home to dinner many years ago when Mama was young.

"I was your age then," she told me. "And I felt just like you do now." "Oh Mama, how do you know how I feel?"

"By looking at you," Mama replied. "Your cheeks are pink, your heart is racing."

"Oh, stop!"

To my surprise, William seemed drawn to me. As soon as Grampa or Mama walked out of the room, he would take my hand in his. Outdoors, as soon as we were out of sight of the house, he would pull me to him and give me a hug. We held hands as we walked through our farm into the meadow behind it.

That was how we spent that winter. William rode his horse Dancer up to our farm on Saturday, arriving midday. He stayed with us for supper, and that night he rode into Market Town to stay at what folks called *the poor man's inn*. On Sunday morning William came back to our house for breakfast and Sunday dinner. Then he left us to ride Dancer for hours and hours back to Birmingham so he could be at work on Monday morning.

"I think he likes you," Grampa said.

Every time William said goodbye and rode off towards Birmingham, my heart sank. I dreamed about him every night. I did my farm chores—feeding the animals, milking the cows, collecting the eggs, bringing in firewood, and going to Market Town to manage Berta's greenhouse. But all I could think about was William. One Saturday he arrived several hours late. I was sure he had found someone new. When he finally got here he told me his horse had lost a shoe, and he had had a long wait at the blacksmith's.

In February, William handed me a heart-shaped box of chocolates, and asked me, "Will you be my valentine?"

"Yes!" I shouted happily.

A few weeks later, William and I went on a walk in the meadows behind the corn fields. I pointed at my secret hideout, the ledge high up where I used to spend hours talking to the wind. But William didn't seem interested in my secret hideout. He said he was too *grownup* to climb up to that ledge, and he didn't want to get his school-teacher clothes dirty.

William worried about getting dirty? I was glad we had been courting during the winter so he didn't see how dirty I got working in the fields. But I wondered, "What will William think of me when I'm covered with mud?"

Grampa and Mama loved William. "Such a gentleman," said Mama. "What a fine man, *a school teacher*," said Grampa.

I complained to them that William didn't like getting muddy. "We need to teach him about dirt farming," said Grampa.

Next time William and I walked in the meadow, he pointed to my secret hideout. "Your Grampa tells me you're a tomboy," he teased.

"Good thing I am," I told William proudly. "It helps get the farming done."

"Your Grampa invited me to your spring planting, so I can learn about dirt farming. Is that okay with you?"

"Yes!" I shouted with glee.

William pulled me to him, hugging me gently. He kissed me lightly on the forehead. Then he said, "My friends and relatives warned me about people up here in north Alabama. They say half of the folks in these hills are Indian savages—they're outlaws hiding from the Indian Removal Law.

"But," William added, "I think your folks are good, decent people."

I stood there, hardly hearing his words, because I wanted him to kiss me again. Then he gave me a long, delicious kiss. And he looked and me and said, "Willow, will you marry me?"

"Yes," I whispered. My heart soared. This beautiful man wanted to marry me!

William took my hand in his, saying, "As tradition requires, yesterday I asked your grandfather for your hand in marriage. He told me that you are a strong-willed young woman, and that *you* are the one to say yes or no." I laughed at my grandfather's words, thankful that he saw my right to decide who I married.

"Where will we live if we get married?" I asked William

William answered with a question. "Where do you want to live, Willow?"

"Here," I said. "My parents need me to keep the farm going."

"Good," replied William, "That's what your grandfather said to me, and it's what I want, too." Then William kissed me again. "I will look for a teaching job up here. But meanwhile, I will work in Birmingham and come up here for the weekends."

For several days I walked around with my head in the clouds, feeling warm and loved. Then one morning I woke up with a start—what had William said about "Indian savages"?

The next day, I went to work with Berta. Together we were preparing the garden for spring. I told her about William's marriage proposal, and she congratulated me. Then I told her about William saying that half the people living up here are "savages, outlaws hiding from the Indian Removal Law."

Berta stood up, stretched, and looked at me. "Deciding to marry is your decision. You, and *only you*, take the vow of *till death do us part*. Now is the time to ask William all the questions you have."

Then Berta asked me some questions. "Does William like to call people insulting words? Or was he just telling you what someone else said to him?"

I told Berta I had never heard him use insulting words before.

"When William comes to your spring planting, watch how he relates to Mr. and Mrs. Henry and their young nephews," Berta advised. Berta's idea was a good one because I know that what people do shows how they feel.

When William came up for the spring planting, he wore old work clothes. He laughed when I complimented him. "You must think I'm a city slicker," he said. "I usually wear old clothes on the weekends, but I've been wearing my Sunday-best clothes 'cause I was courting you."

I introduced William to Miz Mildred and Mr. Henry, and their nephews. All that week, I watched William closely, and he acted okay. I saw him and Mr. Henry talking about horses. I saw William work side-by-side with Simon and Daniel. I heard them laughing together.

In the evenings, after supper William and I took walks around the farm. One day we even climbed up to my secret hideout. We talked about lots of things, but it was hard for me to bring up his comment about *savage Indians*. Finally, when we were up in my spot on the ledge, I asked him if he thought the human beings who lived here before the Europeans came were savages. William insisted that he didn't generally use words like *savage*, and that he was just repeating what his friends had said. Then he apologized for offending me. He said that he liked how our family respects all different types of people.

I still didn't know how to tell William I was Chickasaw. I heard Grampa telling William about his family history—as if it were *my* family history! I was betrothed to William, who knew nothing about me being Indian. He didn't know I had been adopted, and my Chickasaw relatives still lived in a hidden village in the north Alabama hills.

When I saw Berta a few days later and told her that William got along well with the Henrys and got just as dirty as the rest of us. I told her that I didn't say anything about being Indian or being adopted. I asked her "Do you think I should tell William that my birth mother was Chickasaw?"

"Sounds like a secret," said Berta. "I don't like secrets," I replied.

"But you are good at keeping them." Berta winked at me. "Many wives—and husbands—have a secret or two that they keep from their spouses."

Meanwhile, Mama was planning the wedding. "We don't have money for anything fancy," she said. "So we will have a small family wedding here at our home." She had a list of about twenty-five family and friends to invite. She included William's mother, father, brother, and several friends. I told Mama that William's parents were both dead. That weekend, I spoke to William about him inviting his brother and a few close friends. He responded that he would try to locate his brother. But no friend or family of William's ever made it onto the invitation list.

Mama and I talked about the list every day. Henry, Mildred—and Molly, Tiny, and their two children—were on the list. "What about Berta?" I asked. Mama wrote down Berta's name. I saw that Mama's list did not include my real grandmother.

I asked Mama about my grandmother, and she paused. "We promised Auntie Annie to raise you as a white girl," Mama said, "and we have done our best. William, your betrothed, believes you are my child. Grampa told him you were born in this house. So William does not know you are an adopted Indian."

Mama got up and puttered around the kitchen. She kept talking without looking at me. "If Auntie Annie comes, she will stand out. She does not have proper Sunday-go-to-meeting clothes. She looks like an Indian hiding in the hills. William may wonder who she is and have questions. It's your decision, Willow. You let me know what you want to do."

Mama left me standing in the kitchen while she went outside to bring in laundry from the clothes line.

I imagined Grandmother Annie coming to the wedding in her rough clothes and old moccasins, with long braids and brown skin. Mama was right—she would stand out.

I talked to Grampa, and he took a long time before answering me. Finally, Grampa said, "When William asked me about our family, I said you were Mama Rose's child, born in this house."

Grampa asked me what I had told William. "I haven't said anything to William about being Indian, or about being adopted," I replied.

I thought for a while. "I guess Grandmother Annie should not be invited," I told Grampa, "but what can I say to her? How can I tell her?"

Grampa answered, "I think you should tell Annie about the wedding *before* it happens. She's been very good to you, and you need to tell her the truth."

How strange this was. I was supposed to tell Grandmother Annie *the truth* that she couldn't come to my wedding in order to protect *the lie* that Grampa had told William about Mama Rose being my birth mother.

The next week, I went to work for Berta and told her that she was invited to the wedding, but Grandmother Annie was not. I told her that Grampa and Mama were lying to William about me being born to Mama.

"Ouch—that is a pickle!" she said. "But it is up to you, no one else, to tell William *your* truth. You can tell him whenever you decide to—before, or after, the wedding."

I dug in Berta's garden for a while. At break time, Berta brought out tea and told me she just got some news. "Your Chickasaw cousin, Misty, is marrying Gus. Remember Gus? The farm boy you met when we went up there?"

"Of course, I remember Gus." I replied. "His family's barn blocks the trail to Annie's village."

"It is wonderful!" Berta threw up her hands like people do in church. "You and Misty—cousins who both lost your mothers. And now you both are getting married."

"How is Grandmother Annie?" I asked.

"Good news!" Berta said, "Annie has regained her strength and is up and about her village. But her rheumatism still prevents her from walking far."

"It's been so long since I've seen her."

"Yes," said Berta. "But she is alive and feeling better, so hopefully your paths will cross."

I wanted so badly to see Grandmother Annie. I wanted to invite her to my wedding. I blurted out to Berta, "I want to invite Misty and Gus and Indian Annie—and all of my Chickasaw cousins. It's my wedding and I want them to come!"

Berta raised her eyebrows, giving me a look like she thought I was crazy. She suggested I think this through before doing anything. We sat in the warm afternoon sun, and I ranted and raved about the whole situation.

Then Berta held up her hand for me to stop talking because she had something to say. "Often weddings are more for the bride's parents than for the bride," she said. "It's tradition to get married in the bride's home, or the bride's family's church. It's tradition for the mother-of-the- bride to choose who gets invited."

Berta paused and then asked me a question. "Are you planning to stay living in your mama's and Grampa's house? Or are you planning to move to Birmingham with William?"

"I am going to stay here. I need to keep our farm going."

"Well, then, you need to give your Mama Rose and Grampa some consideration," Berta declared. "Let them decide who is invited to your wedding."

We were silent for a time. Then Berta added, "It's true that Mama Rose and Grampa kept your birth mother secret—but that's what Indian Annie asked them to do. And frankly, Willow, you have gone along with it. You can pass for white or for colored, and that makes life a lot easier for you."

Berta told me to imagine the wedding if I invited my Chickasaw relatives. Then think about the wedding if they were not invited. "Sleep on it, take a day or two before you make your decision," Berta advised me.

I thought about it the rest of the day. The next morning I woke up realizing it would be a terrible thing to invite my Chickasaw relatives because it might hurt their efforts to stay hidden. I decided that Mama's list was who we should invite.

In May, Mama mailed out the wedding invitations, including one to Berta but not one to Annie or Misty. A week later, when I went to work in Market Town,

Berta told me she was looking forward to attending my wedding.

Then she told me that Misty had visited her to buy herbal seedlings. "You should expect a visit from your Chickasaw relatives someday soon," Berta said. "Indian Annie is coming down with Gus and Misty to introduce them to your Grampa. It means you can talk to her in person about your wedding."

I felt excited about seeing my grandmother. But I also dreaded telling her that she wasn't invited to my wedding.

On a Sunday afternoon a few days later, William left us after dinner to head back to Birmingham. Soon after he rode off, I saw Gus and his horse and wagon pull up in front of our house. Misty and Gus helped Grandmother Annie get out of the wagon. Sitting on the porch, Grampa greeted them. Mama went out to meet them and then she went next door to the Henrys.

I heard Grampa tell my grandmother that I was in the kitchen. Misty and Gus stayed on the porch chatting with Grampa. I could hear them laughing.

I greeted Grandmother Annie, seeing her for the first time in years. She looked older and limped when she walked, using a walking stick. But her eyes still twinkled, and she spoke with vigor. "I heard the good news— that you found a good man and are getting married. Congratulations!"

"Oh, Grandmother," I said, "I feel happy and sad at the same time."

She asked me about William. I told her that he came from a poor family, and his coal miner father died when he was a child. He went to public school and became a schoolteacher in Birmingham. And he hoped to get a job teaching around here.

"He's white," I told her. "And he thinks I'm white. I wanted to invite you and Misty and Gus to my wedding, but William doesn't know I'm Chickasaw. I've been too scared to tell him. Grampa told him that I was born to Mama Rose here in this house."

I paused. "I hate these lies. I want to go and live in your village with you," I cried. I couldn't stop the tears. I put my head on my arms on the table and bawled like a baby.

Finally, Grandmother Annie spoke. "Willow, listen. It was very hard for me to give you up. But when I found your wonderful Grampa and Mama Rose, I decided I had to give you to them. And I told them to raise you as a white girl to keep you safe.

"It all turned out better than I imagined," Annie continued, "because, for many years, I was able to walk down here to see you. That was wonderful. Then you came up to see me when I was sick. I knew you were in the village even though I was too sick to see you. I felt your spirit, Willow. You helped me get well, and I thank you for that."

My grandmother sat with me, and I kept crying. Then she declared emphatically, *"I do not want to go to your wedding.* It is too hard a trip. I would be out of place. But I will think about you and send good wishes to you."

We sat together in the kitchen, but I still couldn't stop weeping. Then my grandmother scolded me, saying, "You seem weak and confused today. These white families—even the good ones—teach their women to be weak. They don't understand that women are strong and clearheaded."

She reached her hand out to me, and lifted up my face. "Willow, you are a strong Chickasaw woman, just like your mother. My parents taught me to be tough, and that's what I taught my daughter. Our Chickasaw way is to respect strength in our women, the way we respect it in our men. You must remember this as you face challenges today and in the future."

That afternoon in the kitchen, my grandmother convinced me that I was strong and I need to act that way. Ever since that day, when I have a problem I think back on Indian Annie and say to myself, "Willow, you are a strong Chickasaw woman."

The wedding date was set for mid-June. The preparations were enough to drive me crazy. Mama tried to get me to stop farming, saying it was ruining my finger nails.

"Mama," I told her, "I'm a farmer for life and a bride for just one day."

She bought me a pair of work gloves and made me wear them. The day before the wedding, she cut my finger nails and used the nailbrush to get out every speak of dirt. She scrubbed my poor hands so hard they were raw. Finally, she placed Berta's comfrey salve on my poor sore fingers. Thankfully, Berta's comfrey made my skin calm down.

The night before the wedding, Mama washed me and my hair in the big laundry tub in the kitchen. When the sun came up the next morning, it was my wedding day. Mama braided my hair in two long braids, which she wrapped around my head. "Beautiful," she said when she finished. She gave me a new dress to put on for the hours before I would put on my wedding dress.

I felt like a chicken—all scrubbed and dressed, and ready to be put in the oven!

Out in our front yard, I watched Molly with her new baby son Johnny and her daughter Harriet. I hadn't seen Molly since her little boy was born. I wanted to run out and hug her.

Then my brother Thomas arrived. I hadn't seen him for years and years. I wanted to say hello, but Mama wouldn't let me go outside. I watched my brother help Mr. Henry set up a table under the big oak tree and set out a dozen chairs for the wedding.

When I complained about staying inside, Mama gave me presents—a nightgown, bathrobe, and slippers—all packed in a new overnight bag. As the wedding guests began to arrive, Mama led me into my bedroom and helped me put on the wedding dress she had sewn for me. It was white, trimmed with lace, with a lace veil to put on my head. I put on these silly little white shoes, thinking about all the money spent on these ridiculous clothes that I would only wear for one day.

I was afraid Mama was going to make me sit in my bedroom alone until the ceremony began. But she decided to let me go into the living room, as long as the groom did not see me. I felt like a show horse. I kept repeating my grandmother's words to myself, "You are a strong Chickasaw woman." It helped me get through the day.

The weather was lovely—warm with a gentle breeze. Mama had done all the cooking ahead of time, and the kitchen was full of covered dishes. Mama's sister, my Aunt Daisy, arrived with her husband. She had baked a bunch of desserts, and she helped Mama set up a buffet on the sideboard in our living room. Then Molly and Tiny came into the house with more food, and I finally got to see their new baby boy.

More people arrived and mingled. Mama's preacher came. I stood at the front door watching the people assemble in the front yard. The preacher put a white cloth on the table under the oak tree and placed his Bible and cross on the cloth. "That makes it an altar," Mama whispered to me. Then the preacher told the people to find their places. Older people sat on the chairs, and younger folks stood. I saw Miz Mildred, Mr. Henry, and Berta sitting together near the front. Most of the young people stood to the side, where I saw Molly and Tiny and their children.

Everyone got quiet. My brother Thomas appeared from the shadows. He graciously shook my hand, and kissed me gently on the forehead. Thomas had finally learned some manners! Mama handed me a bouquet of flowers, and then Thomas took Mama's arm. Slowly, Mama and Thomas stepped down the front steps into the yard and walked down the pathway to the alter.

Thomas helped Mama sit down on the chair closest to where the preacher stood.

Then I finally saw my William, looking dapper in his new black suit. He walked in and stood next to the preacher.

All eyes turned towards me. A soprano soloist from the church choir stepped forward, opened her arms towards me. She began "Here Comes the Bride," and sang powerfully without an organ or piano. With great elegance, Grampa took my arm. As the soprano continued singing, the preacher nodded to us. Grampa and I walked slowly down the steps and crossed the yard to stand in front of the altar. Grampa let go of my arm, leaving me standing next to William, then sat down next to Mama.

The preacher looked at William and me, and started talking. Most of his words are a blur in my mind. I mainly remember William and me each reciting our marriage vows: *In sickness, and in heath, for richer or poorer, until death do us part.*

Then William put a little thin gold band on my finger. The preacher declared us man and wife and said, "Now the groom may kiss the bride." William gave me the tiniest, sweetest kiss, and whispered to me, "Just a little kiss now. Later is Part Two."

Then everyone cheered—and relaxed and partied. People talked, kids ran around, everybody ate. As soon as Mama's minister left, the alcohol came out. I saw William drinking and talking to my brother Thomas like they were longtime buddies.

William was having a good time chatting with my relatives. Eventually, guests started leaving, and I got to sit down and eat some of Mama's good food. I looked around for the Henrys and Berta, but they had disappeared. I ate and realized that I was exhausted. I went to my little bedroom and saw that Mama had laid out yet another new dress she had made for my honeymoon. I took off my wedding dress and put on the honeymoon dress.

Then Grampa told me and William, "Your coach is ready." The coachman was Mr. Henry, of course, and he took us to the Market Town Inn, the fanciest place around here. It probably cost a week of William's salary. But I was glad to go because it meant William and I would finally be alone.

Our room was beautiful, with a big double bed in it. As William had promised, "Part Two" was lovely. The next day, we had a lazy Sunday, sleeping late, eating lunch at the Inn, and strolling through the town park. At two o'clock, Mr. Henry picked us up and drove us back to Grampa and Mama's house.

I was exhausted, barely able to stay awake to eat. I excused myself and sat in the comfortable chair and must have dozed off. Mama woke me, "Daughter, don't you want to say goodbye to your husband?"

In my sleepiness, I thought, "Why would I want to say goodbye to my husband? We just promised to be together till death do us part."

Then I remembered he had to go to work tomorrow. I woke up in time to watch William get his horse out of the barn. I couldn't believe he had to ride to Birmingham to work the day after our wedding. Wiping sleep from my eyes, I went to William. He gave me a little hug and kiss, and then got on his horse. I stood there watching William's back as Dancer swished her tail back and forth over her rear haunches. *Swish, swish, swish, clop, clop, clop.* Dancer and William headed down the road.

What were those marriage vows about? Yesterday we vowed to be together for our whole lives—and today he was already leaving me.

CHAPTER 21

Grampa and the Deep-Woods Men

T HE WHOLE NEXT WEEK, I felt tired and sad. I missed William. Mama said it was normal to feel let down after all the wedding preparations. "Just take it easy for a few days," she said. So I wandered around the farm, wondering where William was and what he was doing.

I also felt sad about my brother Thomas, who I hadn't seen for so many years. He had been charming at the wedding, gracious to everyone, joking with Molly and Tiny, walking Mama down the aisle, and talking to William. But he said hardly a word to me. After the ceremony he shook my hand and kissed it, saying, "Congratulations!" Then he had some food and drink and disappeared.

That week I found myself thinking about Thomas. At age eight, he had moved to Birmingham to live with Uncle Andrew Fields and Aunt Frida on their plantation. A year later, he came home to Pine Hill for the summer and found me, an orphaned Indian baby, clinging to his mother. I tried to imagine what he felt. No wonder he resented me. I never got to know my brother; our lives went in different directions. Thomas did well enough in his studies to be offered a job in a big law firm in Montgomery, the State Capital. Two years after I got married, he got married, and he invited us to his wedding. But Montgomery is three long days of travel south of here. Mama and Grampa went to his wedding, but I didn't because I was pregnant.

On Wednesday morning after my wedding, Mama said, "Today you get the last of your wedding presents." She stated that William and I needed a private bedroom in the house, and that Molly, Tiny, Grampa, and Mama were solving that problem with *big presents* for us.

Molly and Tiny came over, and we climbed upstairs to the unfinished second floor of our old house. Tiny checked the flooring and decided the bed should go in the center of the room, where the floor was most solid. Tiny took some measurements and brought over lumber to build me and William a frame for a double bed. This was the first time I saw Tiny's excellent carpentry work. The bed he built was his and Molly's wedding present. Grampa's present was a thick, covered mattress to be delivered the next day in time for William's return from Birmingham. Mama gave me a new set of sheets and towels. By the time William arrived on Saturday, we had a nice, private bedroom.

William and I quickly settled into a routine. Monday through Friday, William worked in Birmingham and I pulled weeds in Pine Hill. On the weekends he traveled to see me for a too- short visit. I quickly realized I was married to a man I hardly knew, and who knew little about me. But how I loved him! We had no problem with the loving part of our marriage.

Before the wedding, I assumed that William would help us farm in the summer. Instead, he continued his weekly commute down to the big city. "It's summertime," I told him, "Pine Hill school is locked up in the summer. "What are you doing now that school is out?"

"I am stocking the schools in twelve rural counties with the proper text books, notebooks, pencils, papers," he answered. "I review the curricula for each grade in each school and meet with the principals. My job at the Education Office is year-round."

Before we married, William told me he would look around Pine Hill for a teaching job, but I don't know if he ever looked for a job up here. Maybe he did, maybe not. He just told me there were very few public schools in the north Alabama hills.

Mama called ours a *weekend* marriage. We spent only thirty hours a week with each other. I tried to get advice from Mama, but she simply answered that I had vowed to be with William *till death do us part*. And she reminded me about the murder of her husband. I stopped trying to get advice from Mama.

When I went to work at Berta's, I got to talk with her. "What a lovely wedding," Berta said. I told her that I was sad—I missed William during the long weeks before our very-short weekends.

"Child," Berta replied. "You've been through a lot— the death of your birth mother—never being able to see your own relatives. That's a lot."

I poured my heart out to Berta, mostly complaining about William. She asked me, "Does William share his pay check with you and help out with your family's living expenses?"

"Yes," I said. "He is paying our land taxes. Since Grampa hurt his foot we've gotten behind, and William is making payments to get us caught up."

"Well," said Berta, "sounds to me like you got a good man who's helping your family keep your land. You need to stop fretting." Berta was right about William sharing his money with us.

The next weekend, I asked William questions about his life in Birmingham. "Where do you stay in Birmingham?"

"The Education Office has a bunk bedroom for teachers who live far away," he answered. "Can you take me down to meet those folks?" I asked.

"Sure," he said. But I never did meet those people.

Instead, I got pregnant. In late summer, I started throwing up in the morning. Mama said to me, "Looks like morning sickness to me—bet you're carrying my grandchild!"

I didn't know anything about pregnancy or babies because I had always been the little kid around here. Mama gave me advice: "The first three months are when women are most likely to miscarry—or lose the baby. It's best not to tell anyone until you're more than three months along."

I threw up for three months and then told William I might be pregnant. He was thrilled.

In August, Molly and Tiny came to stay with Molly's folks for a vacation. One hot day Molly, Tiny, their kids, and I were hanging out at the pond. Harriet and little Johnny played in the mud, just like Molly and I used to do. Then Molly announced a big surprise—she and Tiny had decided to move back to Pine Hill.

"I can't believe it!" I told her, "I thought you loved Birmingham. Why did you change your mind?"

"I can sum it up in one word," said Tiny. "Land."

Then Tiny gathered up Harriet and Johnny to take them back to the house for lunch. It was the first time in a long time that Molly and I had a private talk. "We want to have good land to grow food for our family," she told me as we watched Tiny walking away with the children. "Living here is the only way we can own land. It means we can help my folks, and it's a good place for little kids."

"But the schools are still segregated," I said.

"Yes, they are, and it is a big problem for us," Molly told me. "Harriet has been going to the colored school in Birmingham. But Harriet's teacher, who is my cousin Louisa, has decided to move up to Chicago. Louisa's been offered a teaching job up there, and most of her family already lives up there. My little Harriet wants to go to Chicago with Louisa and live with her family up there."

"That's so unfair for you." I said.

Molly wiped tears from her eyes. "It breaks my heart. But Harriet is stubborn, just like I was. We've got to let her go." The laws that separate the races put a big hardship on Molly and her family. Eventually, all of Molly's and Tiny's school-aged children ended up going to Chicago to live with their Aunt Louisa so they could go to her school.

That summer, Molly and I fumed about the cruel world we live in. We also shared good news with each other. "Molly, I think I'm pregnant," I told her. "I know I'm pregnant," said Molly.

That September, Tiny took Harriet up to Chicago and stayed two weeks to help Harriet adjust to living in a big city. Molly stayed in Pine Hill, and we spent a lot of time together. We watched our bellies grow and bet on whose baby would be born first. Together we went to Berta, the greatest midwife for miles around. Molly was my best friend again— we were both married, living next door to each other, and sharing the happy-and-hard-times of motherhood.

William continued to be a city boy, oblivious to the farming life. But he was thrilled about becoming a father. That fall I told William that every October our family worked with the Henrys to harvest the crops, just like we worked together to plant in the spring.

William said that he couldn't take off time from work that fall. That left us short-handed. Grampa could not work, because he was short of breath, hardly able to walk. Even though Molly and I were pregnant, we had to work hard that harvest. Thank goodness we had the Henrys' nephews Simon and Daniel to help us.

After the harvest Grampa got chilled, and no matter how much wood we burned, he stayed sick. The swelling in his feet moved up his legs. He stayed in bed all day long. He couldn't walk, so Mama got him a potty chair, and she gave me the job of emptying it and cleaning it. It was a stinky job, but I loved my Grampa.

Mama brought Grampa's meals to his bed and stayed with him most of the time. My Aunt Daisy came to visit her father every other day. When Daisy left and Mama was busy, I sat with Grampa.

One day Grampa told me he needed to talk to Mr. Henry, so I went to fetch him. When Mr. Henry came over, Grampa told me it was a private matter, so I closed the door behind me.

They talked for a long time.

The next night, Mr. Henry brought over two deep-woods men in rough old coats and boots. They went into Grampa's room and closed the door. After a long time, Mr. Henry opened the door and called me to come into Grampa's bedroom. As I entered the room, Grampa told the deep-woods men. "This here's my granddaughter,

Willow," Grampa said proudly. "She's carrying my great grandchild!"

The men nodded to me. Then they left Grampa and went out to the side yard, where the family tombstones are. I stood by the window, and watched the two men as they looked around.

One man was much older than the other, maybe they were father and son? They lingered out there talking in a strange tongue, which I think was Chickasaw. The younger man squatted on the grass and rolled a cigarette, lit it, and shared it with the older man. Mama saw me staring out the window and told me to stop spying.

The next morning Grampa was in good spirits. I brought him breakfast, hoping he was getting better. But he only sipped tea and wouldn't eat any toast. "Who were those men?" I asked him.

"One is a childhood friend of mine, the other is his son," said Grampa. "Now let me rest." And he slept all afternoon. I brought him soup for dinner, and he said, "God bless you, Willow. Take care of my great grandchild."

That night, Grampa died. Mama had stayed up, sitting with him, but when she dozed off he died. The next morning, I couldn't stop crying.

But Mama was all business that morning. She went next door to ask Mr. Henry to take a message to Aunt Daisy that Grampa had passed. Then Mama wrote a note for me to take to her preacher. It said,

Dear Preacher McDonald,

Judge Jack Farrell died last night peacefully in his sleep. The family wishes to have a house funeral

tomorrow. Can you come over tomorrow after-noon to lead a short service?

We have already arranged the burial by old friends of the Judge, which will take place later in the day.

Sincerely,
Rose Farrell Fields

The weather was cold that morning, and when I tried to put on my winter coat, I couldn't button it over my growing belly. I could feel the baby kicking me, like a little tadpole growing into a frog. Mama gave me her coat, which was big enough for me to button. As I walked to Pine Hill, the baby settled down. I gave Mama's note directly to the preacher, and he told me he would be at our house tomorrow in the midafternoon.

When I got back home, Mama and Aunt Daisy were in Grampa's bedroom, preparing the body. That meant they were washing Grampa and dressing him in his best Sunday suit. I sat and stared into the fireplace. When Mama and Aunt Daisy finished, I was allowed to go into his bedroom. Grampa looked like he was just taking a nap. I couldn't believe he was dead.

I started crying, and Mama hugged me gently, saying, "A few tears are okay, but we have no time for a big cry now—too much work to do. We've got to get the house ready for the funeral tomorrow." We worked into the night cleaning and cooking.

The next afternoon, people arrived and viewed the body. Many cried, and Mama and I cried with them. I recognized some people from Pine Hill School, including children, now grown, who Grampa had tutored. Others I did not know. Some came from Market Town, and there were some old men who were Grampa's Unionist friends from the Civil War. Preacher Davis came with a bunch of Mama's church friends.

The preacher led a brief service, and people sang "Nearer my God to Thee" and other hymns. Many shed tears. When the service was over, people ate Mama's pies and Aunt Daisy's cakes. It was dark when people went home.

Mama and Aunt Daisy and I sat in the living room and ate all the remaining pies and cakes. It was pitch black outside when we heard a knock at the kitchen door. I went and opened the door. It was the two deep-woods men I had met a few days earlier, with two other men.

"You are the granddaughter, right?" said the man who was Grampa's childhood friend. I nodded and invited them in. The old man did not want to come in. "We have come to bury your Grampa," he said. "Long time ago, when I was young, I helped bury your great grandfather. Now we will bury his son, as your Grampa requested. You and your mama say your goodbyes while we dig."

I followed the men to the side yard cemetery, and they started digging a hole. The older man told them what to do, speaking in the strange language. Then he came over near me, and together we watched the men dig.

"Are you speaking Chickasaw?" I asked him. "Yes," he replied.

"I was born Chickasaw..." I started to say, but the man interrupted me.

"I know," he said.

"Do you know my grandmother, Indian Annie?" I said.

"Yes." He replied.

"Are you from her village?" "No."

Then he went back over to where the men were digging. The ground was soft from all the rain, and it looked like they had dug a half-sized hole. I didn't know what the old man said to the younger men, but then he came and talked to me. "We need your Grampa's chair," he said.

"Okay," I said, wondering why they needed a chair. He followed me as I went back to the house. Mama and Aunt Daisy were sitting in the living room. "They want Grampa's chair," I said.

Mama pointed to the chair at Grampa's desk, near the front door. The old man picked up the chair, and went back outside. I followed him. "Why do you need a chair?" I asked him.

"Some Chickasaws like to be buried in chairs, looking west towards the setting sun. We buried your great Grampa down near the Abookoshi River, sitting in a chair. And your grandfather asked to be buried the same way. Your Grampa was a good man, a good friend to the Chickasaws and we want to do what he wishes."

Mama called me back inside, and we said our goodbyes to Grampa. Grampa was still lying in his bed, looking like he was taking a nap in his Sunday-go-to-meeting suit. Mama, Aunt Daisy, and I each kissed him. We told him what a wonderful father and grandfather he had been to us.

Then the Chickasaw men came in to his bedroom, wrapped his body in an old blanket, and carefully picked him up. We followed them as they carried Grampa out to the yard. The hole still looked too small for a full-size casket. But the hole was deep, and Grampa's chair was sitting at the bottom of that hole. The men carefully placed Grampa's body in the hole, so that he was sitting in his chair, looking towards the mountains. Then the old man asked us to leave.

The next morning, I went out to see Grampa's grave. They had put all the dirt back in that hole around him. They had placed a nice big stone on the dirt on top of his grave. Mama showed me some flower seeds that she was saving for me to plant next spring on Grampa's grave.

By the time William came home for the weekend, Grampa was dead and buried. Molly said, "He died happy, knowing you were pregnant with his great grandchild." Mr. Henry said, "I want to die the way he did, suddenly, surrounded by family and friends." William said very little.

CHAPTER 22

Motherhood

I MISSED GRAMPA EVERY DAY. A few months later, William and I moved our bedroom from the rafters down to Grampa's old room, a better bedroom for us when the baby arrived. I liked sleeping in Grampa's bedroom. I had lots of dreams about him.

One day, Mildred asked me to come over to her house to talk. "Your family needs to do more farming in the coming growing season," she grumbled to me. "You need to talk to that able- bodied husband of yours—now, so he can put in a request for a week off in the spring. That's the way city folks do it. Next spring you're having a baby, and we need your husband to help with the planting."

That weekend, I told William we needed to have a serious talk. I thanked him for paying the back taxes for the land and then explained to him how our family and the Henrys always took a week to plant together, and another week to harvest together. It was how we had food to eat all these years. At first, William was testy. He felt that paying the taxes was enough for him to do. I told him it was a big help for our family. But we also needed food to eat, and we had always farmed with the Henrys. This spring we were going to be short of labor because Molly and I were both having babies.

William disagreed. I persisted. It was our first argument. "Okay," he said finally. "I will put in for a week's vacation in April."

"It's good to learn how to argue," Miz Mildred told me approvingly.

That winter was cold, and I could not work at Berta's because I was pregnant and Berta wouldn't let me travel to and from Market Town. I ended up helping Mama make lots of cornbread and jelly, which we sold to the grocery store. I missed William and was jealous of Molly. Her carpenter husband was building their new home for them and their children right next to the Henrys' house. Most days, Tiny worked at home, building his house. Even when he traveled to do carpentry work, he came home to his wife at night.

Molly and I both got bigger and bigger through that winter. One night in late March, I got pains. The next day, Mr. Henry brought Berta to our house, and she stayed by my side through the whole ordeal. Birthing that child tore me up, almost killed me. It took two full days for that young'un to come crying into this world. Berta saved my life, helping me through. Then she put this beautiful baby boy in my arms. "The first is the hardest," said Berta. I was exhausted. I couldn't imagine going through childbirth again.

I looked at my beautiful little one, and the name "Jed" came into my mind. William had missed the whole drama of the birth. When he came home that Saturday, he was thrilled to hold his son. "His name is William Brown, Jr." he said, writing down that name in the bible he gave me when I got pregnant. I kept calling the baby Jed, and William kept calling him, William, Jr.

That baby grew up with two names. Ultimately, it was Jed himself who decided that his name was Jed. We started calling Mama Rose—Gramma Rose. She loved that baby boy and all the others that followed.

That spring planting, I put my month-old baby in a shawl, and tied him to my back. Molly was huge with her unborn child, and we did our best to plant the corn together. We were very happy that Simon and Daniel were helping us with the harvest. William stayed with us that whole week, and I taught him a few things about farming. Tiny and William enjoyed talking to each other, and they hung out together in Tiny's workshop, next to the house he was building.

A few weeks after the spring planting, Molly's baby came. Berta came to help Molly with her birth, but she only stayed four hours. "Molly's a pro, I hardly did anything," said Berta, assuring me that my next baby would be easier. Molly and Tiny named their third child Al, after Tiny's father.

Berta and Molly were right, birthing babies got easier. I got pregnant again and again and again. Jed ended up with three little sisters: Rosie, born in 1891; Alice, born in 1893; and Margaret, who arrived in 1894. After my fourth child in five years, I was ready to quit. But then I got pregnant again. I was weak, and working too hard—I got sick. Instead of gaining weight during my pregnancy, I lost weight. The baby was born dead, and I, too, almost died.

We had another sad family funeral for that unnamed child, burying him in the family cemetery. That summer I was too weak to do much farming, our vegetable crop was small, and a summer drought hurt our cornfields. The winter of 1896 was a hungry one. We had little to eat other than store-bought dried rice and beans. But we pulled together and got through it. My two older children, Jed and Rosie, spent more time over at Molly and Tiny's house than at ours.

Mama Rose helped take care of my two little babies so I could rest.

I told William four babies was enough. William was good for a while, and I recovered my health. But then I got pregnant again and again. Jerry arrived in 1898, and Howie in 1899.

"That's it," I said to myself.

The years went by. Mama Rose loved those babies, especially the girls. She took my daughters under her wing and taught them to love cooking. Jed became best friends with Molly's sons, Johnny and Al. Time seemed to race by—farming, nursing, feeding, washing endless diapers and dirty clothes. William came home faithfully every Saturday and left every Sunday. And he took a week's vacation every spring and fall, to plant and harvest. He and Tiny became good friends, and as our family grew, William hired Tiny to build two bedrooms onto our house, one for girls, the other for boys.

My life revolved around my children. There were so many of them, it was hard to keep up. I saw Berta when I was pregnant, and will be forever grateful to her. I missed talking to her and working in her greenhouse. She was always with me when my babies came into this world, and she would tell me about the young girls who had replaced me working for her. Berta also told me about the doings of my relatives up in Indian Annie's hidden village. I really wanted to visit Grandmother Annie.

One summer Berta and I worked out a secret plan to go to Indian Annie's village. It was the summer after Rosie was born, when little Jed had just learned to walk. William had to travel to Montgomery for an education conference that would last more than a week. Berta needed to deliver seedlings up to Annie's village and pick up harvested herbs. Berta's driver, Mr. George, drove Berta, Jed, Rosie, and me up to Annie's village.

Grandmother Annie was in good spirits. Misty and my other cousins took care of my babies while Grandmother Annie and I sat outside and talked for hours. It was perfect weather, and we enjoyed that afternoon. I think back to that visit often, because a year later Annie passed away.

CHAPTER 23

Secrets and Sorrows

WILLIAM GOT SICK THE WINTER of 1905. At first it was just a winter cold. There was lots of bad weather that year—sleet and snow. William stayed in Birmingham for weeks during the worst of it. Then the weather warmed up, but William did not come home.

One day, I got a letter from him. He told me he had gotten sick, and the Education Office had put him on leave until he fully recovered. For two months, he had been staying with an elderly friend who took in boarders. "There won't be any paychecks until I go back to work," William explained to me.

Two weeks later William rode home on his horse. He said he was better, but he kept coughing and he wouldn't eat. I went to Berta's to get medicine for him. I believe that Berta saved my children's lives, as well as my own.

Berta asked me a lot of questions. She told me that William might have consumption, also called tuberculosis. She explained that, if someone had tuberculosis, they could spread it to family members by the stuff in their coughs. She said the tuberculosis could get into the bedding, and whoever slept on that bedding might get sick. She asked me detailed questions about the rooms in our house, particularly about the second floor. I told her the second floor was unfinished, and that no one had slept up there for years.

"You need to immediately move the whole family, except William, to sleep in that unused second floor," said Berta.

I resisted. "You're saying I can't sleep with my husband?"

"That's what I'm saying—if you want to keep your health." Berta barked at me. "Let William— only William—sleep in that bedroom. You need to sleep upstairs with your children. Move up there immediately!"

Berta insisted that I get new bedding for everyone. "You need to remove all the blankets, sheets, and mats—and burn all of it away from the house and yard where the children play."

Berta gave me sheets and blankets, worn but clean, for each of us, saying, "Since I run a boarding house, I end up with lots of bedding." Then she took me to the General Store, where she found pillows and new straw mats. I told her I had only enough money to pay for the pillows, not the mats. Berta paid for the mats, saying that I needed them all right away.

I went home and hauled all the children's bedding out to the far corner of our yard, to our burning area. That afternoon, I made my kids bathe in the pond, and gave each of them clean pajamas, one of Berta's sheets, a new sleeping mat, and a pillow. Then we all went upstairs to sleep. I slept on an army cot in the middle of the attic. My three daughters slept on one side of my cot, and my three sons slept on the other side.

William stayed in our bedroom. Mama refused to move upstairs. "William's never been in my bedroom," she said, "and I'm not going to climb up those stairs to that attic."

The next day, I burned all of the old bedding in the back of the yard. I wouldn't let any of my children help. That same afternoon, Mama Rose washed all the laundry, soaking it in lye soap, rinsing it thoroughly, and drying it in the sunshine.

Berta's cough medicine helped William for a while, but then his cough got worse, and he stayed in bed for many weeks. I gave William my cowbell for him to ring when he needed me. I tried to get him to go to the local doctor, but he refused, saying he needed to go to the doctor for teachers in Birmingham.

In midsummer, William got well enough to sit outside in our yard. There he could watch the kids play and talk to them from a distance. He wrote to the Birmingham Education Office and made arrangements to return there to see their doctor. He asked me to go with him, suggesting we plan to stay a few days. In late August, we packed our things, and Mr. Henry helped me hitch Dancer to our old buggy. On the morning we left, William, dressed in a suit and clean shirt, said goodbye to each of our children. He told them he loved them, walked to the buggy, patted Dancer, and took the reins.

"Wait just a minute," I said, running back into the house. I took a hammer and nails from the kitchen, and quickly nailed shut William's bedroom. I didn't want anybody going in there.

"Okay, I'm back," I said, climbing into the buggy. And off we went towards Birmingham.

As soon as we were out of sight of our house, William gave me the reins, asking me to drive the horse. He took off his suit jacket and wrapped himself in a blanket and put pillows behind his head and back. Several times he started to cough, and quickly swallowed cough syrup. Then he fell asleep. As I drove the buggy down the road, I wondered if he knew he had consumption— and I wondered if he was going to tell me.

Halfway to Birmingham, William woke up and looked around. "How far have we gone?" I told him we still had a long way to go.

"How are you doing?" I asked him.

"Not good," he said. "I need to talk to you. I've been hiding something from you." He paused. A cloud passed over the sun.

"My parents both died of tuberculosis," he said suddenly. "It runs in families. I should have told you before I married you. But I was afraid you would reject me. I really wanted to marry you."

I felt sudden anger well up inside me. I spat out, "You should have told me before we brought six innocent children into this world!"

"I am sorry, so sorry." He wiped his face with his kerchief. "I felt so strong, so healthy, back then," he told me. "I thought I wouldn't get the disease."

We rode in silence. I was furious. Thank goodness Berta had figured out that William had tuberculosis and told me what to do. William wept—the first time I'd ever heard him cry.

Another feeling crawled around my anger—guilt. I, too, had kept a secret from William. Should I tell him about my Chickasaw mother? My thoughts raced back and forth as we continued riding down the road. I felt like there was an angel sitting on one of my shoulders, and the devil on the other. "Tell him you're Indian," the angel said. "No, you don't need to tell him. He'll never find out," the devil argued.

I drove on, aware of the tears falling down my face. The sun was setting and soon it would be dark. I decided, "Yes, I will tell him." It would relieve me of the burden of holding the secret of my birth.

"I've been keeping a secret from you," I whispered, wondering if he was asleep. "Really? You have?" William muttered from under the blankets.

"Do you remember when you told me your friends warned you about these north Alabama hills being full of savage Indians?"

"Did I say that?" William asked, suddenly awake.

"Yes, you did. You said it right before you proposed to me." I paused. "Then you proposed, and I said yes, I will marry you. And I never told you that my mother was Chickasaw."

"Your Mama Rose is an Indian?" said William, suddenly sitting up. "No, not Mama Rose."

"But... your mother... your grandfather..."

A flock of crows flew across the road in front of us. As the sun set, I told William that my Chickasaw mother died when I was a baby. My Chickasaw grandmother asked Grampa and Mama to take in this poor little Indian orphan. My blood relatives still live up in the mountains north of here.

"I am one of those so-called *savage Indians*," I confessed to William. "I didn't tell you because I thought you would reject me."

William laughed, "I never guessed you were Indian. You have olive skin like my mother had. She was Italian, and I assumed you had some Italian in you."

Darkness fell, and I had to give my full attention to driving Dancer to our destination. I didn't know if I felt relief from my confession. I felt overwhelmed by sorrow for my husband, for my sweet William.

We got to the Birmingham Public Education Office in the dark of the night. The office was locked up. I drove the buggy to the stables behind the office. I took the harness off Dancer, and fed and watered her. William suggested we sleep in the screened-in back porch, which we did.

As we each bedded down on separate couches, William told me that the doctor for teachers had seen him the previous spring and told him he had tuberculosis. This was before William came home, before I had any idea why he was sick. With the Birmingham doctor's signature, William had applied for a place in a sanitarium that cared for state teachers. William had recently received a letter that a room for him had just opened up.

The next morning, the Birmingham School Office custodian came early and unlocked the building so we could clean ourselves before the doctor was scheduled to come. Midmorning, the doctor arrived and met with us. He said that a special coach took patients up to the sanitarium. It was scheduled to pick up William at noon. The doctor had papers for William to sign, and a few for me to sign. William told me something about insurance, but I was so distraught, I didn't remember what he said.

We sat on the front porch, waiting for the sanitarium coach to come. William told me about his goals and concerns for our children. The main one he talked about was

Jed, how he wanted Jed to go back to school so he could become a teacher. How was I supposed to do that? I shook my head but held my tongue, thinking that Jed had all the schooling that Pine Hill could offer. I needed him to help me with our farm. But I kept my thoughts to myself, and William talked on and on.

The sanitarium coach arrived midday. William reached out to me, holding my shoulders at arms' length. He said nothing; his face was drawn, his eyes unfocused. Then he boarded without looking back. There were two other passengers huddled in the coach. One was coughing. William sat down as far from the cougher as he could and wrapped his blanket around him. The coach drove off.

Two large dark horses pulled that coach down the road, and it disappeared around a corner. I just stood there, staring blankly at that turn in the road—watching, waiting, hoping this nightmare would end. But it didn't. William was gone. The sky got dark, and it began to rain.

CHAPTER 24

Life Goes On

I N A DAZE, I WENT to the stable to get the horse and buggy. The custodian helped me hitch up Dancer, chatting about how much the teachers liked William, and how much he would be missed. I couldn't listen—my mind was somewhere else. The custodian gave me some biscuits wrapped in a napkin. I thanked him for his kindness.

I remember little about my ride home. It rained off and on. Everything seemed blurry and far away. Dancer knew the way home—William had ridden her between here and there so many times. She set the pace, and I let her go as slowly as she wanted. It got hot and muggy, but I didn't feel it. I must have fallen asleep in the buggy because when Dancer stopped, it woke me up. It took a moment for me to realize we were still on the road, and Dancer needed water and food, which I gave her. Then we continued on the endless way home.

We pulled up to the house in the dead of the night. Jed ran out, took my satchel, and helped me out of the buggy. I noticed how much he looked and moved like William. Jed helped me to the house, then he took care of Dancer.

In her bathrobe, Mama met me at the door. "You look like a ghost," she said.

I thought bitterly, "We all become ghosts sooner or later." But I held my tongue—it was no time for joking. Wordless, I went straight to bed and fell fast asleep.

I dreamt I was riding, riding, riding in a ghostly carriage, led by a horse I couldn't see, down a long and dusty road to an unfamiliar destiny. Had I trusted too much in the turning of the wheels? Had I trusted too little? Had I gotten home--or was I still on the road?

I woke in daylight, not knowing where I was. Then I saw the rafters above me, and realized I was home. My children whispered down in the kitchen. Scattered across the attic floor were kids' mats, pillows, blankets and dirty clothing. I lay there thinking about all the urgent things that needed to be done—decontaminating William's bedroom, burning all his belongings, washing clothes for the whole family, getting ready for the new school year. And, most important, our fall harvest. We needed to eat this winter.

Still in bed, I saw Alice's sweet face appear from the stairwell. "Mama, you must be hungry," she said. "We got some good vittles down here for you."

Slowly, I put on my bathrobe and climbed down the stairs. I was hungry, and Mama served me my breakfast favorites. I watched Mama telling my daughters what to do. She looked old, sitting there on a chair with her feet up. But she continued to feed my children.

I remembered how sorrowful Mama was when I was young, sad about her husband's death and about her young son leaving home to live with his rich relatives. Yet every day of my life, Mama Rose got up and prepared breakfast, lunch, and dinner for Grampa and me. And she still cooked for me and my children. Mama seemed happier now than when I was small, she loved being a grandmother.

"I need to be more like Mama Rose," I thought to myself. "Just do what is needed for us to survive." After I finished my breakfast, Mama and I were alone in the kitchen. I thanked her for caring for the kids while I was gone. Then I headed out to the field to check on our crops.

Jed was by himself, hoeing in the cornfield. "Where is Dad?" he asked me.

"He has tuberculosis," I said. "He's at a sanitarium, which is like a hotel for people who have that disease. It's in the mountains east of here, and they feed people healthy food and encourage them to get fresh air."

"When's he coming home? When can we go see him?" he asked.

"Son, I'm sorry, but we cannot visit him. We don't want any more exposure to that disease. Your father will come home only if he gets well, and no one knows when that will be," I said, looking into my son's sad brown eyes.

"But," I added, "You can write letters to him. I have his address. Your Dad would love to hear from you, and I am sure he will write back to you."

Jed talked to his brothers and sisters about writing notes or drawing pictures for their father. That day I noticed my younger kids were not nearly as sad about their father as Jed was. Jed was the only one who had gotten close to William.

The next morning, I went back out to the cornfield to talk to Jed about the harvest. He told me that woodchucks had eaten up our vegetable garden. "Simon shot two of them, and Mildred cooked up some woodchuck stew," Jed told me. He also gave me the dates Molly had set for the harvest. Molly's sons, Johnny and Al, were coming down from Chicago to help.

"Sounds like you are our family's head farmer!" I told him proudly.

"No Mama!" declared Jed, "I don't want to farm any more. I want to go to school in Birmingham to become a teacher like my dad!"

"Son, I need you here," I told Jed. "Our family needs you." "Mom, I gotta teach. I promised Dad."

"Then the rest of the family will starve," I said. This argument with my oldest child lasted for years.

Several nights later, I lay on my attic cot until I could hear all my kids sleeping. I tiptoed down the stairs, removed my nightgown, and put on an old long-sleeved shirt, long skirt, and raggedy gloves. I found a bar of lye soap in the kitchen and put it with my nightgown on the back porch.

I took the hammer from the tool box and pried open the nails that held William's contaminated bedroom door shut. I tied a handkerchief to cover my nose and mouth like a bandit. Then I went into William's bedroom and gathered up his clothing, sheets, towels, and rags—and wrapped them up in his bed sheets. I tied it all into a large ball of dirty stuff, opened the bedroom window, and tossed that big ball out onto the grass.

Then I went outside, picked up those contaminated things, and carried them to the burn area. It was a warm night with a full moon. I built a fire and burned all of William's garments and bedding. The moonlight helped me carry out my work. Folks call the big moon *the poor-man's lantern*. I remembered Grandmother Annie telling me stories about Grandmother Moon, who guides the women. A feeling of calm came over me as I tended the fire.

When I finished the burning, I took off my raggedy clothes and burned them as well. I walked to the back porch, naked, and picked up my clean nightgown and soap. Still naked, I walked in the moonlight down to the pond. I lay in the warm pond water, bathing my body and hair. The pond water felt good, and I lay there for a long time, looking up at the moon.

"Thank you, Grandmother Moon, thank you, Grandmother Annie," I whispered. I suddenly felt an urgent need to tell my children about their Indian ancestry.

Under the first lights of dawn, I put on my clean nightgown and walked back to the house. Jed and Mama were in the kitchen, eating breakfast. I told them what I had done and warned them that the room itself was still contaminated. As Jed got up and headed to the cornfield to work while it was still cool, I got out the hammer and nailed the bedroom door shut again.

Mama and I planned our next big chore: washing all the dirty clothes for our family. We usually did laundry every Monday, but we had missed several weeks, so our plan involved participation by the whole family. We discussed it at dinner that night. The next day, Jed and Margaret hung up extra clothes lines from the trees in the back yard. Then they built a fire and started heating up water in the big pots. Rosie and Alice set up our three washtubs on the lawn, one for the first wash, another for the second wash, and the third for rinse. They secured our hand wringer to a table in the yard, so we could wring out the clothes before hanging them on the clothes lines.

Each family member washed, rinsed, wrung out, and hung up their clothes to dry. Little Jerry and Howie got help from the older kids, and we all laughed when the little guys tried to hang up their clothes on the low-hanging ropes.

After all the clothes were washed, Jed and Margaret laundered all the sheets. Meanwhile Rosie, Alice and I mopped and cleaned the girls' and boys' bedrooms, and wiped down the bunk beds and dressers. Then all the kids put on their old swimming clothes, and went down to the pond to bathe.

It was a hot, sunny day. By late afternoon, the girls took the clean, dry laundry off the lines, and brought it in to the big table in the living room. Everyone helped to sort and fold the clothing, and then each kid put their clean clothes into their own drawer in the dresser they shared in their newly-cleaned bedrooms.

We put clean sheets on all the beds. All the kids slept downstairs in their clean bedrooms, except Jed, who told me he was fifteen years old and didn't want to share a bedroom with his five- and six-year-old brothers. I had to continue sleeping in the attic, because the bedroom I had shared with William was still contaminated. I thought I would be alone up there, but Jed insisted it was where he, too, would sleep. He moved his sleeping mat as far away as he could from my cot and hung a sheet between us. He took great pains to avoid talking to me.

That fall, I looked at my "to do" list every night, and made plans for the following day. I worked hard, but it kept me from worrying about the future.

One day, Jed came running to me with a letter from the mailbox. "I got a letter from Dad!" he said, smiling.

Then he ran off without telling me what William had written. That night, he read his father's letter at the dinner table and talked to his brothers and sisters about mailing something back to their dad. For several days, Jed helped his younger siblings write notes and draw pictures.

Jerry and Howie were so cute—they did everything together, including drawing a picture of themselves. Jed put the boys' drawing and the notes from each of his sisters in a big envelope. I gave him the pennies to buy postage stamps from the Pine Hill Post Office.

"Jed would make a good teacher," Mama Rose said. I nodded, but said nothing.

The first day of school was fast approaching. All my child between six and twelve were supposed to go to school. Jed and Rosie had finished school. Alice and Margaret were returning to school, and Jerry (age six) was about to start school. But poor Howie, at five, was too young, even though he was just as tall as his brother.

Jed told me that, when he was in school, there were two little boys a year apart. Their mother resourcefully registered them as *twins* so they could go to school together. I figured this was worth a try, so I walked down to Pine Hill School and registered my two boys as twins. Problem solved.

Each school child needed a nice outfit for the first day of school, a family tradition. Rosie took charge of getting the first-day-of-school outfits for her sisters, and Jed for his brothers. Rosie took her two sisters to the church rummage sale, and they came home with several school outfits each. Jed went next door and talked to Molly, who sent him home with a box of little boy clothes that her Johnny and Al had worn. Molly had saved them for years for Jerry and Howie.

On the first day of school, I walked with Alice, Margaret, Jerry, and Howie to the Pine Hill School, the same schoolhouse I had gone to so many years earlier. I remembered how that place used to scare me—a room full of kids could quickly become a battleground. Once I had friends with me, it was much easier. I was happy that my daughters and sons had each other.

October brought the fall harvest, and Jed was thrilled when Al and Johnny arrived from Chicago. Molly and Jed were in charge of the harvest, and they put everyone to work. Jed headed up the boy crew of Al, Johnny, Simon, and Daniel. They were all strong and energetic, and brought in the corn crop in record time. Molly led my three daughters and her two nieces in the vegetable harvest. I worked with them, and saw some new friendships developing. Mr. Henry, walking with a cane, supervised little Jerry and Howie in digging up sweet potatoes.

Mama and Mildred provided the meals. It was a big crew and a bumper crop.

After we finished the harvest, Jed headed to Birmingham with Al and Johnny to go to harvest celebrations. Then Al and Johnny went back to Chicago, the nieces went back to Birmingham, and my children went back to Pine Hill School. My kids complained about their teacher being boring, but they still liked to go to school to see their friends.

Mama and Mildred prepared the harvested crops for storage and sale. Molly and I prepared the fields and gardens for the cold season. We women took stock of the harvest. The good news was we had enough food for both our families to get through the winter. The bad news for my family was we didn't have enough cash to pay our land taxes.

Jed returned from Birmingham grumpy as an old donkey. "I'm sick of farming," he said. "I'm near sixteen years old, ready to be out on my own. I want to live in Birmingham."

"I hear you, son," I responded. "Figure out some way you can make so much money that we can feed all your brothers and sisters, and pay our taxes." It was the same old argument.

Jed came home one day from delivering Mama and Mildred's pies and cornbread to the Pine Hill Grocery and told us that the old grocer had sold the store to a young man named Pincus Feldman. Jed had just met the new owner, and Mr. Feldman said he would continue to sell Mama's and Mildred's baked goods. He also told Jed he was going to build another room onto the store so he could sell more items and become a general store.

"What kind of name is Pincus Feldman?" I asked Jed.

"Jewish," he said. "I asked him if he needed help at the store—and he hired me! I'm working from dawn to midday, Monday through Friday."

"Good work, son!" I told him and explained that he needed to give me most of his earnings so we could catch up on the land taxes. Jed could keep some for himself, and when we caught up he could keep more of his wages.

Mama and I talked about our financial situation and the danger of losing our land if we couldn't pay our taxes. I told Mama that I could return to doing paid work for Berta in Market Town, but Mama Rose nixed that idea. "This family is a full-time responsibility. When you were away, it near wore me out," she said.

December arrived, and so did Jack Frost—freezing everything. Thank goodness we had already harvested all our crops. Cold weather gloom caught me and wouldn't let go. In the mornings the house was full of kid noise. When they left for school, it was so quiet. Mama Rose and Rosie were home, always working on something together. Mama was teaching Rosie how to sew school clothes for the kids. I loved the closeness between my mother and my daughter, my lovely pair of Roses.

I was lonely and jealous of them. The bitter cold kept me inside with nothing to do. One morning, I put my coat on and knocked on Molly's door. She was alone and invited me in. It was so tidy there compared to the chaos of my house.

"I've hardly seen you since William got sick," Molly said. "I miss you. You've had such a hard year," she said, heating up water for tea. We started talking and went on for hours. It felt good to share with Molly.

Molly had big news—she was going to be a grand-mother! Harriet, twenty-four years old, was expecting a baby. I hardly knew Harriet, because she had gone to Chicago to live with relatives when she was young. Harriet was a good student, and she became a teacher. But unlike her younger brothers, Al and Johnny, Harriet never visited Alabama.

Molly found it very hard to be separated from her children, and she visited them every year up there. But she couldn't imagine living way up in Chicago. "Now," Molly explained, "I'm gonna be a grandma! And I want to get up there to Chicago and stay all winter to help out my daughter and her baby."

After the baby was born, Tiny planned to travel up to Chicago for a visit. But in the meantime, he would stay here because he had carpentry work through the winter. For a moment, I worried that Molly would stay in Chicago. But she assured me that she would be back by spring. "Because," she told me, "farming is what I do."

And, being Molly, she had plans for Pine Hill when she came back for the warm season, "I want you and me to teach a circle of girls—your daughters and my nieces. We could tell stories and teach crafts and farming, discuss life and history and what's going on. What do you think, Willow?"

"Sounds great to me!" I said. "The women around us—Berta, Mama, Mildred—know so many skills, and we can invite each of them to teach the girls different things." It made me think of Berta. I had hadn't seen her since William had left us.

"Especially Berta," Molly said. "She has a lot to teach—precious knowledge, especially for the womenfolk."

When Molly left for Chicago a few weeks later, her parting words to me were, "Go visit Berta. You need her, and she loves you."

Meanwhile, my husband seemed to be enjoying the sanitarium. He and Jed corresponded weekly. Jed got his siblings to write notes and make funny drawings. William, always the teacher, sent back his children's notes with the spelling corrected.

In early December, the kids made Christmas cards, which Jed mailed to their father. We expected a quick response, but nothing came in the mail. Right before Christmas, a nice store- bought card arrived from the sanitarium, but there was no signature on the card and the envelope's address was not in William's handwriting. I took that as a bad sign, but I said nothing. And Jed said nothing. We celebrated Christmas with homemade gifts and a good dinner with the Henrys.

Then one cold blustery morning in January, I woke to find the fire had gone out. I struggled to start a new fire, but there was too much ash in the fireplace. In my rush to shovel the grey powder into the ash bucket, I spilled ash all over myself and my clothes. I was a mess.

Suddenly there was a knock at the front door. There was no time to clean up, so I just opened the door. A blast of cold air blew me in the face and the ashes swirled around in a big cloud, hitting the postman. He was more bundled up than usual, in a scarf that covered his mouth and nose. He handed me an official-looking letter and left without saying a word. Jed appeared suddenly, took the letter, and opened it. He was a faster reader than me, so this was one way he liked helping me. Tears welling up in his eyes, Jed handed the letter to me, ashes falling over his hands.

I read aloud, "William Brown passed away on December 26, 1905."

"No!" cried Jed. "It's not fair!" And he stormed out of the house, slamming the door.

Alone, I read the rest of the letter, which stated coldly that due to the disease, the body would be cremated, and a container of his ashes would be sent to me in a month or so. I knelt down by the cold fireplace. "Ashes to ashes, dust to dust," I muttered. I couldn't remember the rest.

CHAPTER 25

Earth

FEBRUARY ARRIVED COLD, WET, AND windy. Soon it was Valentine's Day, and I remembered those heart-shaped boxes of chocolates that William always gave me. That morning the postman knocked on the front door and placed a plain cardboard box in my hands.

"It's your husband's ashes," he said, turning away quickly without looking at me. I stood in the doorway—holding that box, not knowing what to do.

Mama Rose heard the postman and came into the living room. "Put the box on the mantle over the fireplace," she said softly. "That's a place of respect." Then she suggested we have a family funeral the next day. "We will give William a proper burial," she told me. "Jed can find us a big stone to mark the grave."

That night, at supper Mama Rose told the children the plans for the funeral. The next day was Saturday, so everyone was home. Jed asked for help finding a big stone to mark the grave, and Margaret, Howie and Jerry all volunteered. Rosie and Alice helped Mama prepare a "proper lunch." I went next door to invite the Henrys.

Jed and his crew found a perfect stone and scrubbed it until it was clean. Then they dug a hole, just deep and wide enough for the box of ashes. Miz Mildred and Mr. Henry came over, and we all stood there—my six children looking like stair steps, from small to tall. Mama Rose led us in prayer; she knew just what to say. In a brave, clear voice, she sang "Nearer My God to Thee." I wept through it all.

Then we ate lunch and told stories about William. Mr. Henry described his first conversation with my husband: "I said to William, 'I need to *learn you* how to farm.' Then William looked at me and said, 'Sir, you're not going to *learn me* anything! You're going to *teach* me to farm.'"

"Always correcting us," I laughed. "This is the man who sent his children's letters back from the sanitarium with the spelling corrected!"

Jed looked so sad. He didn't want to hear anything negative about his father, even jokes. He told us about his trips to Birmingham with his dad when he was small. The other children talked about their daddy giving them chocolate candies, organizing Easter egg hunts, and taking them to the County Fair. It was a good day, I laughed more than I had for years.

Dreams came to me almost every night, sometimes sad, sometimes angry. They told me what I worried about— getting the money to pay the taxes, putting food on the table, and keeping Jed home to help me farm.

One evening in early March, Mr. Henry knocked on my door. He looked very formal. "Miz Berta requests the honor of your presence for tea tomorrow afternoon. I'll give you a ride and bring you back by suppertime."

"Let me ask Mama Rose," I responded.

"I already spoke to Rose, and she said it's fine with her," Mr. Henry told me.

The next afternoon, as we drove to Market Town, Mr. Henry said, "I saw one of your Chickasaw relatives who lives in Indian Annie's village."

"Who?" I asked.

"Chief Will," Mr. Henry told me. "I met him twenty-some years ago, when he asked your Grampa and Mama to take you in. Now he is still the Chief, but he is getting on in age. He asked me to give you condolences on your husband's passing. And the Chief invites you to come up to his village for their Spring Equinox. Berta is planning to go, and so am I. We want you to come with us."

Mr. Henry pulled his buggy in front of Berta's house, and I got out. It was wonderful to see her again. We went to the greenhouse and sat in the afternoon sunlight. I started weeping as soon as I sat down.

"Let the tears fall—crying is good." Berta said. "William is in the spirit world. You can talk to him in your dreams and daydreams."

"But Berta, in my dreams I am yelling at him!" Then I told Berta about my last trip with William down to Birmingham, when he finally told me his secret that his parents had died of consumption.

"No wonder you're angry at him!" Berta said.

"I pray none of my children get tuberculosis," I whispered. Berta assured me that I had taken necessary steps to protect them from the disease.

Then I told Berta, "When William told me about the TB in his family, I told him my secret—that my birth mother was Chickasaw."

"Good for you!" cheered Berta. We sipped tea, sitting in her beautiful greenhouse. Then she asked, "Have you thought about telling your children about your mother?"

"No," I answered. "For a long time, I've felt like I should tell them about my Indian heritage. But I haven't figured out how to do it."

We talked about Chief Will's invitation to go up to their village to celebrate the Spring Equinox. "Chief Will really wants you to come up there," Berta told me. "He invited Henry, Mildred, and me—hoping we would bring you."

"I want to go!" I declared. "But what should I tell my children? They don't know anything about me being Indian."

Just then Mr. Henry appeared at the greenhouse door. Berta invited him to join us. "We're talking about how Willow should tell her children about their Chickasaw heritage," she said. "Mr. Henry, what do you think?"

Mr. Henry sat down, and Berta poured him some tea. He said, "The Spring Equinox is coming up very soon. My advice, Willow, is to tell your kids you're traveling to *see old childhood friends*."

"What?" said Berta abruptly. "Shouldn't Willow tell her kids that she is Chickasaw?"

"Yes, she should tell them," responded Mr. Henry. "But there isn't enough time before the Equinox to do it right."

Berta glared at him. We sat in uncomfortable silence. Then Mr. Henry asked me a question, "Willow, do you remember when I told you I was Choctaw?"

"Yes," I said. "We were sitting at the picnic table during our spring planting. I was little."

"Willow," Mr. Henry paused. "Let me tell you what went into preparing for those words I said that day at the picnic table. When you were a baby, when Chief Will came to ask your Grampa to take you in, he also came to see me. Through the Indian grapevine, Chief Will knew I was Choctaw. Choctaws and Chickasaws speak the same language. A long, long time ago, we used to be the same tribe. So Chief Will came to my house, and we talked. Chief Will asked me what I thought about your Grampa and Mama Rose because he wanted fair-minded people to take in this precious little girl. I told Chief Will, 'They're good people.' And Chief Will asked me to watch over you."

Mr. Henry paused and looked at me, "Willow, when you got to be six or seven, I decided it was time to tell you I was Choctaw. But before I said anything, I had conversations with your Grampa and Mama Rose to be sure it was okay with them. Telling someone you are Indian is risky. It might have sounded casual that day at the picnic table, but I put a lot of planning into those words."

I sat there silently, realizing all these years Mr. Henry had been watching out for me—my own guardian angel. I marveled at Mr. Henry's careful way of telling me he was Indian when I was young. Then Mr. Henry said, "Willow, it's a big thing for your children to learn that you—and they—have Indian roots. Some of your kids might chose to ignore this news, others might be very interested. Your Chickasaw heritage is their heritage. But it is still forbidden and illegal."

Berta nodded her head, "Now I understand. Thank you for explaining it, Mr. Henry."

I said, "Mr. Henry, I want to go to the Equinox to see my relatives, and I will tell my kids I'm just visiting childhood friends."

As Mr. Henry and I traveled home that afternoon, he asked me, "Did Mama Rose ever talk to you about your Chickasaw relatives?"

"No. But she did answer my questions. When I was little, I asked Mama lots of questions," I told him.

"Yes, I remember your questions," chuckled Mr. Henry.

As we trotted towards home, I told Mr. Henry, "One time, Mama did lots of talking. She told me the sad story about her husband getting killed. I was old enough to figure out that Mama's husband couldn't be my father because he died a long time before I was born. I've seen our cows mate with the bull, so I knew that calves are born months, not years, after their parents mate. I asked Mama who my father was, and she told me that she and Grampa had taken me in. Then I asked Mama who my birth mother was, and she told me, 'Ask Auntie Annie.'"

As we drove over the Abookoshi Bridge, Mr. Henry said, "Your Mama Rose is a good-hearted woman. I think you should talk to her privately about traveling up to Indian Annie's village. A conversation with your mother is an important step *before* talking with your children."

"Good idea," I told Mr. Henry. Mama Rose needed to know about my trip to the village—and I needed time to figure out what to say to my children.

The next morning, when Mama and I were alone in the kitchen I spoke to her. At first, she wondered why I wanted to travel up to the village, because Indian Annie had died a long time ago. Mama also thought I should *never* tell the children about my Indian relatives. "Everyone sees you as a white girl. Why can't you let sleeping dogs lie? Why do you want to jeopardize your children's futures by telling them that you are Indian?"

I thought about Mama's questions all that day. The next morning, when we were alone I told Mama, "I want to tell my children that I was born Chickasaw because

206

Indian people have traditions and knowledge that are good for all of us to learn. They know how to take care of the land and the wild animals. They know about herbs and how to use them to heal. I want my children to know who I am, and who they are—and that we are connected to people who have lived here for thousands of years."

I finished by saying, "Mama, each child will make up his or her own mind as to whether to ignore what I say or to learn more about it."

Mama was silent for a long time. "Okay," she said. "They are your children."

"And you are their grandmother—thank goodness!" I hugged my Mama Rose, telling her, "You are why we all are alive and well."

Mama liked being appreciated. She said, "Tell me exactly what you tell the children so you and I will be on the same page."

That night, as we sat down to supper with all the children, I announced that I was going with Mr. Henry and Berta to see childhood friends.

At dawn on the Spring Equinox, Mr. Henry and I headed north in his buggy pulled by Partner. We picked up Berta in Market Town and continued onward. Mr. Henry explained that many Indian tribes celebrated the seasons. "It's a way of honoring Mother Earth," he said, "On the first day of spring, they celebrate the Spring Equinox. On the first day of summer, it's the Summer Solstice—the first day of fall, the Fall Equinox—and on the first day of winter, the Winter Solstice."

We traveled quickly towards the Chickasaw village. The road was in much better condition than during our last trip. At the trail to Two Trails Crossing, we got out and walked. Again, we left the buggy with Preacher Jones in his stable.

As we hiked up the trail to the Chickasaw village, I expected to see the big barn blocking the trail to the village, but the barn was no longer there. I wondered why, hoping that it meant relations were good between the Chickasaws and the local whites.

Misty and Gus greeted us. A dozen more kids ran up to us. "Are these little children all yours?" Mr. Henry joked to Misty, looking at more than a dozen little ones.

"I only have two children," laughed Misty. "The other children are my nieces and nephews. Thank goodness they have their own mommies and daddies!"

Gus took Partner to a nearby paddock to graze with several other horses. I looked around the meadow, locating Annie's old log home where I was born and Eve's home next to it. Behind them was a newly built four-room house. An old man came out the door and waved at us. It was Chief Will slowly walking towards us with his cane.

"Perfect weather for our ceremony!" Chief Will declared as he joined us. "Mother Earth is blessing us. It will be a while before we start. Feel free to relax in my house, or sit on the rocking chairs, or wander around."

Mr. Henry and Berta went with Chief Will. I wandered over to a covered shelter in the middle of the meadow where there were two woodstoves back-to-back, and women were preparing delicious-smelling food.

The women invited me to help them prepare a Chickasaw dish called *bunaha*, which is cornbread mixed with either beans or sweet potatoes, wrapped in corn shucks, and boiled in water. They showed me how to take a small handful of a mixture of cornbread with beans, and place it in a corn shuck, and tie it with a thinner corn shuck. They also wrapped the cornbread mixed with sweet potatoes, tying it in the same way. When we finished all the wrapping, we placed all the shucks into boiling water. That's how I learned to prepare bunaha. On the other woodstove a delicious stew was boiling in a huge pot. They told me it was *pishofa*, made from hominy and fresh deer meat from the village men's successful deer hunt. Yum!

By the time we finished cooking, other people had arrived, and Chief Will led us to the place where we were having the ceremony. It looked like the entire village was coming. I counted around forty people, more than half of them children. I saw several more wagons and horses grazing in the paddock. It meant folks who did not live in the village had ridden up here like we did.

We walked towards a grassy area where people stood in a circle. As we walked closer I smelled sage and saw it smoking in a clay pot. We stopped by the sage pot, and a girl with a large turkey feather waved the sage smoke on each of us in turn. "This sage purifies you as you join the ceremony," she told us.

We joined the circle, which grew larger as people arrived. I watched a young man arrange tinder, kindling, and small logs in the fire pit. He stood up and introduced himself as Lowak, the village firekeeper. He welcomed us to the Spring Equinox and began the ceremony by lighting the fire. "We offer tobacco to the fire," said Lowak, "honoring the Creator, hoping the Creator will hear our prayers." Then, speaking in Chickasaw, he placed tobacco leaves on the fire.

Next, an elderly woman introduced herself as the village's Bird Clan Mother. She spoke in Chickasaw offering thanks to the Creator. As she spoke, Chief Will whispered to us that she was giving thanks for the earth, waters, trees, plants, corn, herbs, animals, birds, fish, insects—and for the sun, moon, and stars.

Then Chief Will spoke, first in Chickasaw, then in English. "We welcome you all to our ceremony. Our village almost died out after the Indian Removal, the Civil War, and all the violence of those years. But those of us who survived stayed close to our Mother Earth, and we shared with one another. We had children who had children, and now our children attend the public school in the village down the trail. They are learning to read and write English, and that is good. We also want to preserve our language, our heritage. So we speak Chickasaw in this village and teach it to our children. We also want to share our traditions with our friends and relatives who live outside our village."

Then Chief Will said, "Now, together we will greet the four directions." We turned to face the south, and the Chief said, "Thank you, Spirits of the South, for the return of the warm weather and the awakening of the land and the animals—when the seeds begin to stir from their winter sleep and the buds on the trees begin to swell into blossoms."

Next we faced west, and the Chief thanked the Spirits of the West for bringing us the rains and cool breezes, for bringing the sunset every day, and for bringing the nighttime for rest.

Then we faced north, and thanked the Spirits of the North for their wisdom and for the lessons of winter.

Finally, we all turned towards the east, where the rocky ridge rose up from the land. The chief said, "Thank you, Spirits of the East, for the rising of the sun each and every day. Thank you for this first day of spring, when everything is in balance—cold and hot, night and day."

After the Equinox Ceremony, we were invited to eat a meal together, including pishofa and bunaha. Chief Will told us that all the food had all been grown or hunted, and cooked right in the village. It was delicious. After a lunch and lots of laughing, singing, and conversation, most people headed home.

The Bird Clan Mother announced there would be a small condolence ceremony for the families of those who had recently passed into the spirit world. I walked with Berta and Mr. Henry on a path through the cornfields towards the rocky ridge. The land was quiet and beautiful. A blue jay flew by. "Hello, Tishkila," I whispered, remembering that Grandmother Annie's mother's name was Tishkila, which means blue jay in Chickasaw.

This time we went to a spot near the village's small cemetery, right at the base of the rocky ridge. I recognized the cemetery, because Misty brought me there on my visit many years earlier. We saw wooden benches. "Let's sit," said Chief Will. "My old bones can only take so much standing." There were eight of us, and we sat down on the benches, forming a circle.

Chief Will explained we would speak in turn around the circle. He produced a beautiful hawk feather and held it as he spoke. "For the first go-round," said the Chief, "name the person or persons you have lost." Then Chief Will asked me to begin, and handed me the hawk feather. I named my husband William, who had died just three months earlier. Then I added, "I want to also name my grandmother Indian Annie and my mother Spring, who are buried here in this cemetery."

"Thank you, Willow, our long-lost daughter, for coming to visit us," said the Bird Clan Mother.

Then the old man sitting next to me took the feather. He introduced himself, "I am Ned, and I am mourning my mother Eve, my father Stephen, and my aunt Indian Annie—who was a second mother to me. I am also here to reconnect with my cousin Willow." And he reached out to me and held my hand.

I suddenly realized this was not a circle of strangers—these were my close relatives. They were the people who knew me when I was a baby. My tears fell, and Cousin Ned put his arm around my shoulder.

The circle continued as the feather passed from person to person. Berta spoke about her dear friend Indian Annie and about her own parents, who had been slaves. Mr. Henry mourned for his Choctaw mother, who was forcibly removed to the West when he was young.

Next was Misty's turn, and she named her mother Jenny, who had died giving her birth, and her grandmother Wilma, who was the same age as my grandmother. "Wilma and Annie grew up with each other," Misty explained. "They lived here during the starving years, and they argued with each other all the time. But they also respected each other. I loved them both. Annie told me she needed to be nice to Wilma so that Wilma would repair her torn moccasins. And Wilma told me she had to respect Annie because Annie was the lead farmer in the village."

After everyone had spoken, the Bird Clan Mother took the feather and thanked the mountains, waters, rocks, turtles, and "all the creepy crawlies." She told us to see the earth and all the plants and animals as our relatives. She thanked our ancestors, who had passed on and told us to talk to them, either out loud or silently. She said we should pay attention to our dreams because that's often when the spirits visit us. Then Chief Will took the feather and slipped it into his jacket. He and his brother Ned took out their hand drums and sang a blessing-healing song.

As we walked back to the village, I found myself walking next to the Bird Clan Mother. I told her I liked how she talked to the spirits. I also told her about some of my dreams when I am yelling at my dead husband.

"People often feel abandoned—and angry—when a spouse or parent dies. Your dreams about yelling may mean that you left words unsaid when he was alive."

"That sure is true," I replied. "We both kept big secrets from each other."

"You have an opportunity, even now, to talk to your husband—to tell him things. You can do it while you are awake or while you are asleep."

We continued down the path, and the Bird Clan Mother said, "I am a midwife. I helped your mother bring you into this world." I asked her if she had a regular name or if "Bird Clan Mother" was her only name.

"My name is Sissy," she answered. "I knew Indian Annie very well. She was my elder cousin, and we did healing work together."

Suddenly I remembered Annie's stories about a young midwife named Sissy, who was a wise healer. I loved Annie's stories, but I was never sure if this Sissy was a real person or an imaginary character. Now I knew—I was holding hands with a powerful medicine woman.

I asked Sissy about the Bird Clan, "Can I join the Bird Clan?"

"You are already in the Bird Clan," remarked Sissy. "Everyone born in this village is in the Bird Clan because we were all born from the two sisters who founded this village almost a hundred years ago. All your children—boys and girls--are also Bird Clan. I am your Clan Mother."

I stood there, stunned. Sissy added, "Welcome home, Willow."

That night we ate supper with Chief Will's family. After dinner I talked to Ned, Chief Will's younger brother. He told me that Indian Annie had told him the story of her life, and that he had written it down. Ned said, "Annie talked a lot about you as a baby—and walking down to visit you after your Grampa and Mama Rose took you in."

"I want to read Indian Annie's story." I told Ned.

Ned promised that if I came to the Summer Solstice Ceremony in June, he would show me Indian Annie's book. He also said they had a storytelling circle, where people worked on telling their own stories. I told Ned that I would love to join the circle.

"Your grandmother was a wonderful storyteller," Ned said. "Her words still help us teach our children our history and traditions."

That night, Berta and I stayed with Calvin and Nellie Jean in their farmhouse, and the next morning, Mr. Henry joined us for breakfast. Then we left for home. As we traveled I thought about my relatives in that village, how they revered the land and worked together to survive—and gave thanks for everything. I thought about what Bird Clan Mother told me about dreams and talking to spirits. I wondered if I could be part of Ned's storytelling circle.

As we got closer to the farm, I struggled to turn my thoughts to my home. What was I going to tell my children about being Indian? Learning the secrets of my ancestry was helping me make sense of my experience—and I wanted to know more. How could I keep the farm going when what I really wanted to do was to keep coming back again and again to my birth village?

CHAPTER 26

Summer Solstice

HOME ON THE FARM, I weeded every day and dreamt every night. Following Sissy's advice, I tried speaking to William's spirit when I was awake and alone. I thanked him for all our children, telling him how each was doing. I imagined William, the education official, chuckling when I told him how I lied that Howie and Jerry were twins so they could go to school together. I described how Rosie and Alice always helped their Grandma Rose, and how Margaret was a tomboy, like I used to be. I complained about my arguments with Jed, because of how much Jed wanted to be a teacher, but stressed to my dead husband that I needed Jed on the farm.

It was comforting to talk to William. My dreams got calmer and my mood more cheerful. I realized I did love my husband.

I thought long and hard on how to tell my children about our Chickasaw heritage. It became urgent because I wanted to go back up to the village for the Summer Solstice and hoped they would come with me. I told Mama Rose I would talk to the children on Sunday while she was at church. That morning at breakfast, I told the children I wanted to tell them about my trip to see my childhood friends.

After breakfast, as we sat at our big table in the living room, I began, "I was born in a Chickasaw village north of here in the mountains. My mother was Chickasaw, and her name was Spring."

"But Mama Rose is your mama!" blurted out Margaret. Suddenly all the children looked at me and began listening harder to what I was saying.

"Mama Rose *is* my mother, but not my birth mother," I explained. "My birth mother was Chickasaw, and her name was Spring. She died when I was a baby."

That started more questions: "Are you sure, Mama?" "Who is *my* birth mother?" "Are you *really* our mama?"

It took a while to answer their questions. Finally, I was able to continue, "When I was a baby, times were very hard. My Chickasaw relatives were starving. My grandmother found Grampa and Mama Rose, and asked them to take me in."

My children looked at me in surprise. "I was lucky," I told them. "I was adopted by the most wonderful mama in the world!" That, my children could agree with.

Then I told them about my recent trip with Mr. Henry and Miz Berta up to the village where I was born. I met cousins who remembered me as a baby. Now, like me, they are grown with children of their own. Their children are going to the nearby public school to learn to read and write. In their village, they are also learning their Indian traditions and history.

Then I told my children, "I will answer any questions you have."

Some of their questions reflected the lies people tell about Indians: "Do Indians steal chickens—do they steal corn? Are Indians savages? Weren't you scared to go up there? I answered them as best I could.

Fortunately, my children knew some kids in school who had confided in them that they had parents or Gramparents who were Cherokee or Chickasaw or Choctaw or Creek.

After they ran out of questions, I told them we all were invited up to the Chickasaw village for the Summer Solstice on the first day of summer in late June. I told them it was a celebration of the season, and I planned to go and take whoever wanted to go with me.

"Who wants to go?" I asked, looking at six pairs of eyes filled with surprise. No one said yes— no one said no. I guess my story was a lot to take in. I assured them that they still had time to decide to go with me this June or at another time in the future.

The next day, Margaret helped me out in the fields. To my delight, my eleven-year-old daughter told me she wanted to go with me to the Summer Solstice. That made me very happy. I knew Margaret would have a good time.

Meanwhile, Jed was not at all interested in the Chickasaws or any other Indians. In the days that followed we continued to argue. He made me angry, but he continued to give me most of his earnings, and I was able pay our land taxes. Jed and Molly organized our spring planting, and we had a good crew, Molly's family and all my kids.

The planting went well until the day after we finished. That morning my temper flared. Jed, Molly, and I were supposed to plan the summer farming, but Jed was nowhere to be found.

"Your son and my boys left for Birmingham this morning at dawn," Molly told me. "What?" I yelled so loud that Mama Rose and my children looked at me with alarm. "It's okay," said Molly. "Jed told me what we need to know."

Storming out of the house, I headed for the pond. Molly called after me, "Stop, Willow! Let's talk."

As I got to the pond, I burst into tears. Molly caught up, and we sat on our rocks like we used to do when we were girls. "You've had such a hard year," Molly said. "But don't take it out on Jed. He's working hard, and …"

"I need him to head up the farming!" I cried. "How can we eat if he runs off?"

"Jed is being responsible," Molly said. "He is working hard and giving you his earnings. But he has dreams—just the way I did. And he's lost his father, who was his hero."

"We have to eat." I whispered. "How can I keep the farm going by myself?"

"You're not *just by yourself*." Molly raised her voice, waved her hands at me. "You have me, my nephews, and all your kids!"

Molly paused, letting that sink into my thick skull. "Remember back when it was just the five of us—you and me when we were little kids, and my parents and your Grampa? We always found a way. Your kids are getting bigger, so they can help more and more."

I realized I was shaking with rage. "Why am I so angry?" I asked Molly.

"Your anger make sense to me," said Molly. "You husband lied to you about his family's illness. Then he died on you, leaving you with six hungry mouths to feed."

"I don't know what to do," I whispered. "I want to go north and live with my Chickasaw relatives. But I can't because of those six hungry children."

I sat on my rock, and anger flooded over me. "Jed is young and strong, and he knows how to farm," I muttered. "But he wants to run off and abandon us."

"Willow," said Molly, "Remember when I went through my teen years? Remember how terrible I acted? I yelled at my parents and gave speeches like they were children!"

I laughed, remembering Molly's speeches.

Molly was serious, "Your Grampa helped me. He said to my parents, 'Put yourself in Molly's shoes.' And it was hard, but my folks tried to understand how I felt. And we worked out with a way I could spend time in Birmingham. I think you should try to put yourself in Jed's shoes. It won't solve the whole problem. But it might help to work out a compromise."

We sat for a long while, and I calmed down. "Okay," I muttered. "I'll try." Then Molly and I went back up to the house, where we sat down and planned the summer farming based on what Jed had suggested to Molly.

The next few days, while Jed was away with Johnny and Al I thought about ways to ease the tension between Jed and me. I decided to move back to the first-floor bedroom and leave the attic to Jed. I had to thoroughly clean out William's sick room. I took the hammer and pulled out the nails that locked William's bedroom door shut. I hauled his mattress out to our burn area, chopped it up, and set it on fire till nothing was left but ashes. Then I thoroughly washed out that bedroom with lye soap and water. I decided to continue sleeping on my cot. Tiny helped me bring it down from the attic to put in my newly cleaned bedroom. Then he dismantled the bedframe he had made for William and me, and we carried it up to the attic to store.

Jed, Johnny, and Al came home from Birmingham, and Molly's sons left on the train back to their jobs in Chicago. Jed discovered that he had the attic to himself, and he thanked me. I told him about my talk with Molly and how I was trying to put myself in his shoes. Jed said that Molly had also talked to him, and he was trying to imagine what I had been through. For the moment, at least, Jed and I were getting along.

Soon the Summer Solstice approached. Margaret and I decided to spend two nights in the Chickasaw village. On the first day of summer, we left at dawn. Margaret asked to drive Dancer, and I sat next to her in our buggy. Margaret confided in me that she loved horses, and her best friend at school said the Chickasaws were good at raising horses. Margaret decided she wanted to have a horse farm when she grew up. "That's a good idea," I told her.

We got up to the village by midday. Misty and her twins, Winnie and Danny, met us and invited Margaret to join them for lunch. "Yes!" said Margaret, and she skipped off with Winnie. Misty told me that Chief Will, his brother Ned, and Sissy wanted me to join them for lunch. As I walked across the field to Chief Will's house, I saw Clan Mother waving to me from the front steps.

"How are you?" Sissy said, giving me a warm embrace.

"Glad to be here." I said. After lunch, Sissy and I sat down on the grass. She asked me how things were going, and I told her about my talk with my children. Sissy laughed out loud when I told her about my kids' questions about my birth and adoption. I also told Sissy about my arguments with Jed, and how Molly told me to put myself in Jed's shoes.

"Good advice," said Sissy. "If you push too hard to keep a teenage child, he—or she—will just leave. It happened to me. My daughter and I argued, and then she left home. Next time I saw her, she was married and pregnant!"

"I depend on Jed too much," I told Sissy, who asked me about my other children. I told her about my three girls—two of them, homebodies—and the youngest, Margaret, my horse- loving tomboy, who had come with me to the village.

"It's wonderful that Margaret came with you," said Sissy. "Next time, I bet she'll bring a brother or sister with her."

Then she added, "Margaret sounds like a good one to teach to lead the farming," telling me that Chickasaw women have always been the lead farmers. "The white man thinks that women should just stay in the house—how ridiculous!"

"You sound just like Indian Annie," I remarked. "Thank you," said Sissy. "She was my teacher."

Joined by Will and Ned, we walked over to the center of the field for the Solstice Ceremony. People were gathering there, and I caught a glimpse of Margaret running with Misty's daughter and a bunch of other kids. The kids joined us for the ceremony, which ended with drumming, singing, and what they called a *stomp dance*, where they followed the dance leader running in circles around the meadow. Then we had a delicious feast. As the sky grew dark, people lit a big bonfire and danced some more. Then Margaret went with Winnie to sleep at Misty's house.

I stayed overnight at Chief Will's house, because I wanted to read my grandmother's story. There were only two copies of it; the second copy was at Ned's house many miles away. No one was allowed to take Indian Annie's story out of the Chief's house, so I needed to stay there to read it. As soon as I settled in the house, Cousin Ned handed me a large composition notebook titled *Indian Annie, A Grandmother's Story*, written in Ned's clear handwriting.

"It took Annie and me the whole summer to put that story into writing," explained Ned. "Every day, your grandmother talked to me, and I wrote her words down. The next morning, I read to her what she had said the day before, and she corrected it. After we finished the entire story, I copied it into this notebook. Later I copied it into another notebook, which is at my home in Florence, Alabama."

That night, I sat in a comfortable chair at a table with an oil lantern in the Chief's guest bedroom. I read my grandmother's book. Every chapter made me cry or laugh. Sometimes both. When I got to the chapter on my mother's death, I knew I had to stop. I turned off the lantern, climbed into bed, and fell asleep. Dreams swirled around me. The only thing I remember was this feeling of love, a mother's love, a grandmother's love, and my love for them.

When I woke, it was morning. I lay there thinking about Indian Annie. Her story connected me so deeply to this village and to all these relatives I was meeting. I felt grateful to Ned for writing down Indian Annie's story so that I could read it. And I realized I was thankful that Grampa and Mama Rose pushed me so hard to learn to read.

I heard quiet voices in the kitchen. I had slept late, and no one had bothered me. There was a small table in my room next to the bed with a pitcher of water, a bowl, and a small birch twig for me to brush my teeth. I washed up and dressed quickly.

No one was in the kitchen, but there was a note next to a piece of cornbread. "Cornbread and tea for Willow," the note said. "Add hot water from kettle to make tea." I fixed my tea, picked up my cornbread, and wandered out the front door. Sissy sat in a rocking chair on the lawn, and I sat down next to her in an empty rocker.

We watched children playing tag across the big field. I saw Margaret outrunning the boy who was *it*. Margaret was a good runner, just like I used to be.

"Sissy, are any of those children yours?" I asked.

"No," she responded. "My kids grew up on our farm miles from here. I wish they had grown up here. My daughters married local farm boys, and I have three grandchildren. I also have a son who is farming down at our farm with his dad today."

We sat quietly, watching the children. "It's so peaceful here," I mumbled. And I must have dozed off.

Suddenly I heard yelling. As I woke up, I saw Sissy, cane in hand, moving as fast as she could towards the children. I saw a grown man near the children waving his arms and yelling. He was pointing at my Margaret!

I started running to Margaret as fast as I could. I heard Sissy yell, "Jeremy stop!"

The grown man, his face full of rage, was still yelling at Margaret, who was running away from him. Suddenly the man sat down, and put his head in his hands. Was he crying?

Panting hard, I finally got to Margaret and cradled her in my arms. I saw Sissy, on the grass holding the big man who cried like a baby. Then the man pointed again at my daughter, "Stranger!" he yelled. "What's she doing here?"

Misty pulled Margaret and me away from the group into a nearby log cabin and closed the door behind us. My heart was racing. Who was that man yelling at my daughter? I put my arm around Margaret, holding her tightly. She was shaking.

"Margaret, what happened?" I asked her.

"Everyone here is so nice," Margaret cried. "Then suddenly, out of nowhere, this big, scary man comes and starts yelling at me!" I hugged her hard, thinking that I cherished my children more than anything in this world. I felt the dreams of bringing my children to this village fading away.

Misty sat next to us, "I'm so sorry," she said. "Jeremy acts like a little baby." We sat together silently, barely breathing.

There was a knock on the door. I tightened my hold on Margaret. Sissy came in and sat down next to us.

"Margaret, I am so sorry that my son, Jeremy, scared you." Sissy said. "He is twenty-four years old, but he is still a little child. If he doesn't know someone, he gets scared and yells at people. He thinks that yelling will stop strangers from hurting him. Once he knows you and you know him, he is kind and sweet."

I felt Margaret relax a bit. Sissy reached out and took Margaret's hand in hers. "Jeremy had a hard time growing up on our farm down yonder. Kids made fun of him and pushed him around.

That's why he's scared of strangers. Jeremy was supposed to be farming down yonder with his dad today. But something upset him this morning, and he came up to the village looking for me."

Then Sissy looked at Margaret. "Are you okay?" she asked. "He scared me," Margaret mumbled. "He's so big and mean."

I hugged my daughter, but Margaret pulled away from me, sat up tall, and said, "I'm okay. I'm strong and can run fast—away from him!"

Sissy smiled, "I am glad that you are strong and can run fast. But we want to do better than that. We want you to feel comfortable here, not always ready to run. I think it would be good for us to talk to Jeremy when he is ready."

I felt Margaret shiver against my arm. I knew I needed to speak. "Your son scared me, too," I began. "Anything that hurts my child hurts me. Jeremy reminded me of bullies in my school who used to pick on me when I was small. And I must be honest, I will not be able to come back to this village with Margaret, or any of my children, unless Jeremy is ready to tell all of us that he will never scare any other friendly visitors in this village. I love coming here. This was where I was born, and I want to come back here again and again. I want to get to know all of you, and to bring my children with me. But I can't come if I have to worry about Jeremy."

"I hear you," said Sissy. "He must learn not to yell at strangers. But also, we as a village need to include Jeremy in ceremonies—not just exclude him when people he doesn't know come here."

Margaret and I agreed that we were ready to talk with Jeremy, and Misty and Sissy left to find out if Jeremy was ready. Soon they came back with Jeremy and Chief Will's grown son, Jason. We sat on stools in a circle.

Chief Will's son introduced himself, "I am Jason, and I wasn't here this morning, so I didn't see what happened. But I came to talk to my cousin, Jeremy, because I love him as a brother. He and I talked about Margaret, who is our cousin. We both are meeting her for the first time today. There are other cousins and friends who we don't know, but we want them to come visit us. We want everyone to feel comfortable here, not scared."

Then Jason looked at Jeremy, who was sitting awkwardly on a stool, and said, "Jeremy, do you have something you want to say?"

"I- I- I sorry," the big man stuttered. He looked at Margaret, his face shy and sad. "You are my cousin. I sorry." He put his head in his hands and wept.

Holding my hand, Margaret looked at him, searching his forlorn face. Then she said, "Jeremy, we are cousins. Let's be friends."

Then Jeremy's face became a smile. "I am happy, want to be friends," he said.

I was so proud of my daughter's gumption! I said to Jeremy, "I want to be friends with you." Margaret and I talked with Jeremy, who was now friendly and kind.

Sissy told us all, "We are going to make sure my son comes to all of our Solstices and Equinoxes, and that his friend Jason is here with him. That way, if Jeremy has a question or a bad feeling, Jason will be right there to talk with him."

Jeremy smiled, "I like my cousin Jason."

Then Jason said, "Let's go have a good day together!"

We went outside, and there was Gus holding a pony, white with black spots on it. "Margaret, would you like to ride our pony?"

Margaret smiled, "Yes!" Gus lifted her onto the pony. Off she went with Gus and his daughter Winnie to get two more horses so they could ride around the village together.

Sissy and her son came over to me. Jeremy took my hand and again told me he was very sorry. He said, "Auntie Willow, you're my long-lost cousin. Please come back again."

The next morning, Margaret and I prepared to leave after breakfast. "See you at the Fall Equinox!" everyone said.

"Come back soon, cousins!" Jeremy called to us as we left.

As we rode home, I asked Margaret how she felt about the village. She said, "I was scared, because suddenly this big guy is yelling at me. But then I saw Cousin Winnie yell at Jeremy—and I saw Auntie Sissy coming across the field towards us and you running to me. I figured I got people on my side! Then Jeremy said he was sorry—he wanted to be friends, and I wasn't scared anymore. Jeremy's just a big little boy."

Margaret sat quietly as we clipped-clopped down the road. Then she added, "I'm gonna tell Jerry and Howie all about our trip. I bet they will come with us to the Fall Equinox."

We got home, and slept well that night. The next morning at breakfast, the children looked at Margaret. "How was your trip?" they asked.

In a rush of words, Margaret told them all about it, especially about riding a pony named Surefoot. She ended saying, "I can't wait to go back for the Fall Equinox."

Howie raised his hand, like he had been taught in school. "Can I go with you next time? I want to ride a pony."

"Me, too!" Jerry blurted out, waving his hand in the air.

CHAPTER 27

Deep Roots

THAT SUMMER FELT ENDLESS, LONG, and hot. Jed had given us a 1906 calendar for Christmas, which he nailed to the kitchen door. The day after we got back from the Summer Solstice, I counted the days in that calendar until the Fall Equinox. Ninety-one days—it felt like forever.

As I hoed the cornfield I imagined going to the Fall Equinox with Margaret, Jerry and Howie. Those daydreams helped me get through July and August. Jed was working four days a week at Mr. Feldman's store and putting in two days a week in our fields. He told me he wanted to learn carpentry from Tiny, but he would hold off until the end of the growing season. Jed wanted to do anything but farming.

Rosie helped Mama cook and was in charge of cleaning our house. Alice babysat several days a week in Pine Hill and organized our family's laundry. She and Rosie worked together on the cleaning and the laundry. Margaret milked our two cows every day and cared for our farm animals. She also helped me in the fields—a good worker, strong and energetic. Jerry and Howie collected firewood, and Margaret was teaching them how to milk our cows. The little boys also came out in the cornfield with me to help me weed.

One afternoon in midsummer, Rosie and Alice cornered me as I washed mud off my arms and legs in the pond. "Mama, thank you for inviting us to your birth village," said Alice. "But Rosie and I can't go up with you because we can't leave Grandma Rose by herself."

"That's a good reason," I told them. "Taking good care of your grandmother is very important, and I love you for doing it."

Then Alice glanced at Rosie and announced to me, "Mama, Rosie has a boyfriend."

Rosie looked like she wanted to slug her sister. "Alice, mind your own business!" she said.

Then Rosie turned to me, "It's true, Mama, I do have a boyfriend. His name is Fred Hunter, and I really like him, Mama."

"Now, Rosie, you're only fifteen. Don't rush things," I warned her.

"I know, Mama," she hesitated. "I told him about you being Chickasaw, and he promised to keep it secret. Then he told me that his grandfather is Cherokee."

"Indian blood runs in a lot of folks around here," added Alice.

"Yes. Let's learn from our ancestors and be proud of them," I told my daughters, and they agreed.

Summer dragged on. Some days in August it was so hot and dry that even the weeds shriveled up. On the hottest days, I just worked in the mornings and spent the afternoons sitting under the oak tree with Mama Rose, drinking mint tea.

September arrived, and I talked with Mr. Henry about plans to travel to the Fall Equinox with three kids. He told me that Dancer was getting too old for such a long trip. I realized I always thought of Dancer as young and vigorous, but Mr. Henry pointed out that she was over twenty years old.

"You can still use Dancer for local trips, carrying one or two folks in the buggy," said Mr. Henry, "but I'm gonna think on what to do about your trip up yonder with your three kids."

A few days later, Mr. Henry told me he wanted to go with us to the village because he wanted to see his Chickasaw friends again. He could trade with a friend for a wagon and a strong young horse. "That way, you, me, and your three kids could make the trip without wearing Dancer out," he said. I told him that sounded good to me.

As I packed for our trip, I suddenly thought about the blue jay comb that Indian Annie gave me as a child to help me connect with my roots. I had worn it to Molly's wedding, but not to my own wedding because at that time I was hiding my roots. I stopped packing and looked for that comb in my secret hiding place. There it was, covered with dust. I wiped it off and put it in my hair, knowing that from now on I was gonna wear it anytime I wanted to.

We left for the village in the early morning light. Margaret sat up front next to Mr. Henry while he drove the horse. I listened to Margaret telling him about her Chickasaw cousins going to public school in Two Trails Crossing. "Many of the people up in the mountains have Indian mixed into them," Margaret said, "even in Pine Hill, lots of my friends have Indian Gramparents."

Mr. Henry told Margaret, "Where I grew up in Mississippi and Alabama, none of us Choctaws could go to public school. The Choctaws mixed with Negro folks, but none of us were allowed in the schools because they were *white only*. That's why Mildred and I never learned to read—and why Molly's had to send all her kids to Chicago to go to school."

"That's not fair!" said Margaret.

"Margaret, you sound just like your mother." laughed Mr. Henry, "I agree with you, it's not fair."

Once we got up to the village, Misty's kids Winnie and Danny grabbed Margaret, Howie, and Jerry. I saw them talking to Jeremy and Jason. I watched Jeremy intently—happy to see him all smiles.

Soon Chief Will arrived and we all made a circle for the Equinox Ceremony. I stood with Mr. Henry. Across the circle, I saw Margaret standing with Jeromy, Jason, and her little brothers. It made me happy to see everyone smiling.

The ceremony was beautiful and lunch was delicious. After the meal was done, my three children came over to ask my permission to hike around the village with Misty and Gus's teenaged twins. I said yes. It meant I had the afternoon to myself to read *Indian Annie, A Grandmother's Story*.

I read until the supper bell rang. Then I sat with my kids, and they told me about all the animals, plants, birds, and bugs they had seen. Misty asked me if all my kids could stay with them at her house that night. Her twins Winnie and Danny had pitched a tent big enough for all five children to sleep in just outside their house.

After dinner, Ned invited me and Mr. Henry to a small storytelling circle the following morning. We both said we would love to attend. As people prepared for the bonfire, drumming and singing, I said goodnight to everyone and slipped back to Chief Will's house to finish reading my grandmother's story.

The next morning, Ned arrived at Chief Will's house with his wife Talitha. A few minutes later Mr. Henry knocked on the door. Ned offered us tea and cornbread, telling us there would be only four of us in the circle. "But that is good for your first time," he added.

We sat down in Chief Will's comfortable living room, and Ned told us there were many kinds of stories, including traditional stories that teach lessons on working in harmony with the earth and all its creatures. "There are also stories that tell our history," he said, "and journeys that people have taken in life. Storytelling is the way Indian people learn their history and traditions. In the past, before we learned reading and writing, all the stories were told orally."

Ned sipped his tea and continued, "Nowadays, it's more complex, because the Americans have pushed us Indians off our lands and tried to banish our stories. In this village, our children are lucky enough to go to the public school in Pine Hill because this is an area where Indians hid out, and many married white people. When the local whites wanted to build a public school, they needed enough children to get Alabama to provide a teacher. So the locals declared that our children were *white* and invited us to send them to the school. Now our children are learning how to read and write in school.

"But it means," Ned emphasized, "that we must focus even more on keeping our stories and traditions. Storytelling is all the more important." Ned finished his introduction, saying, "Let's go around and introduce ourselves, and tell us what kind of storytelling you want to do."

Talitha spoke next, saying she had been born a slave just before the Civil War began. When the war ended, she and her mother traveled northward to Memphis, Tennessee. "I was lucky enough to go to a school for the colored, where I learned to read and write, and I eventually became a teacher. I got a job in the colored primary school in Florence, Alabama, where I met Ned." Talitha had brown skin and thick curly black hair streaked with grey. She explained that she had both African and Indian blood in her. She met Ned, married him, and they raised three children. All their children got educations but had to leave home to find jobs because there were so few jobs for educated colored people. It meant Ned and she only saw their children and grandchildren twice a year.

Then it was Mr. Henry's turn to speak. "I can't read or write," he said, "but I have a life story that I want to tell. All my grandchildren and great grandchildren live up in Chicago, and they need to know the stories of their elders. It's very important to me because I am old and my days are numbered." Then Mr. Henry stopped talking.

Ned prodded him, "Tell us a little bit of your story, Mr. Henry."

"Well," he said. "I was born Choctaw, just a few years before the Choctaws were forced to go to Oklahoma. My mother knew what was coming and feared for my survival. She sent me with my older cousin to Mobile, Alabama, where we had some kin. I never saw her again. I was so little that I can't even remember what my mother looked like." Mr. Henry took out a handkerchief. "And here I am—still crying about it."

Ned said, "That is the beginning of a powerful story."

Ned nodded to me because it was my turn to speak. "I haven't decided what to write. I was born here, adopted out to a white family. I just finished reading *Indian Annie, A Grandmother's Story,* which is *my* grandmother's story. Now I understand how important it is to write down our stories." I paused, then added, "When Mr. Henry just spoke, he gave me an idea—he can tell his story and I can write it down, just like Ned did for my grandmother."

We continued talking, listening to each other, asking questions, giving suggestions. I realized I was getting excited about a project for the upcoming winter—working with Mr. Henry to write down his story.

Ned thanked us for our ideas, gave each of us a present—a composition notebook like the one Indian Annie's story was written in. "Try to write, or jot down notes, or draw pictures—every day," he said. "Mr. Henry, you can tell your stories to friends and relatives and ask them to write them down in your book."

I sat there holding my notebook, feeling connected to my ancestors and to this village.

Ned told us that we would meet again in six months during the Spring Equinox. "Winter time is storytelling time," he said, "but not a good time to travel up into the mountains because the weather is dangerous. Stay close to your homes and families, and tell stories—that's your winter homework!"

Then we heard small knocks on the door. There were Jerry, Howie, and Jeremy telling us that vittles were ready down in the meadow. After eating, we headed home. My three children giggled in the back of the wagon, and Mr. Henry and I talked as we took turns holding the reins.

Mr. Henry told me how meaningful the storytelling circle had been to him. "I got a pretty good idea what story I want to tell," he whispered to me.

I promised Mr. Henry, "I want to hear all your stories, and I will write down your words in your notebook." Then I added, "I don't know what my story is yet, but I'm gonna be thinking about it."

"Well, when you figure out your story, I'll be there to listen," he said.

We rode down the road in silence. We got home safe and very tired, and the children and I slept late the next morning. After breakfast I tried to reorient myself to Jed's 1906 calendar on our kitchen door. It was September 26, 1906. I was thirty-nine years old. I still had six children to feed, but there would be another trip to the village—my village—in the spring.

The fall harvest was coming up in a few weeks, and Jed and Molly filled me in on the plans. I returned to hoeing every day. School was in session, so Margaret, Jerry, and Howie were in Pine Hill every weekday. In the cornfield, I worked by myself and liked being alone. I could think my own thoughts, day dream, and have conversations with the dead. I cried when I spoke to Spring, my mother. And I laughed when I told Grandmother Annie how much I loved reading her book.

One day in the cornfield, I stopped and looked around. Leaning on my hoe, I told myself, "Got to keep weeding." But something, or someone, made me stop and look across the meadow towards the hill where I used to have a secret hideout. I wandered closer and saw the ledge where I used to go as a child, the place I went to be alone with the wind and sky.

A few days later, I climbed up to that ledge and sat there looking out over our farm and the Henrys' farm, our houses, the woodshed, the pond. "I'm turning forty years old next birthday," I said to myself. "I still have many years ahead of me. I'm in a new chapter in my life, a reconnection with my Chickasaw family."

Then a profound thought entered my head. "I have deep roots in this land!" I cried out to the wind from my still-secret ledge. "This is where I belong and where I will live my life. Thank you, Mother Earth, for giving us all we need!" Then I climbed back down to the field, picked up my hoe, and got back to work.

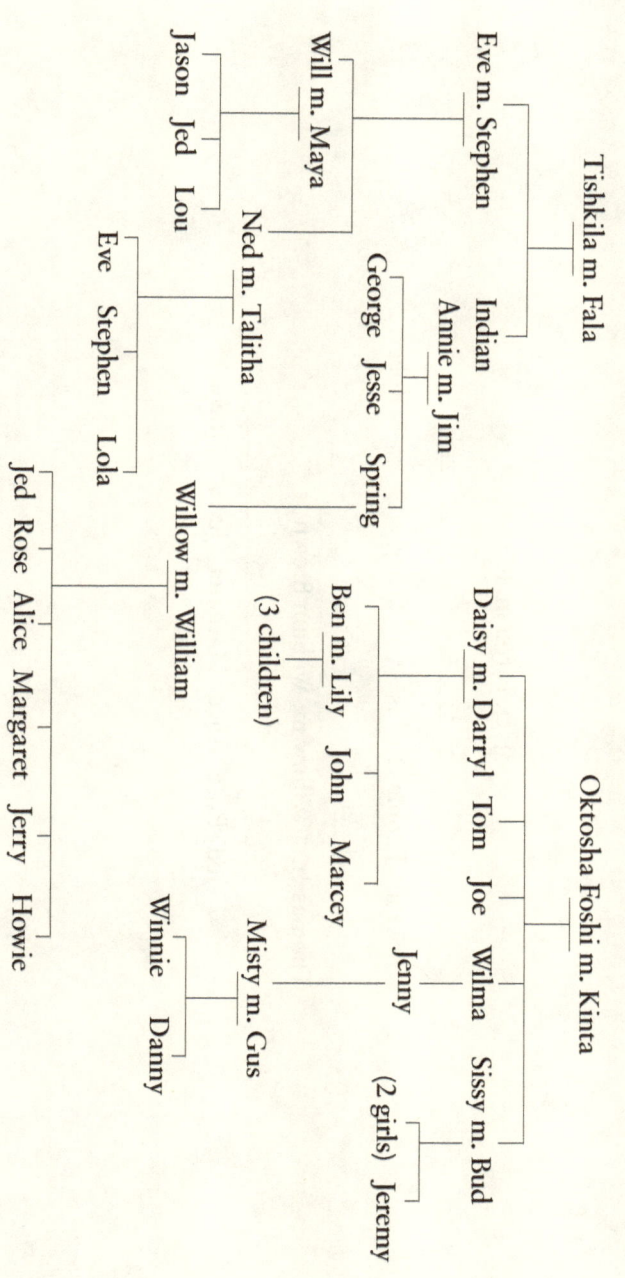

Willow's Chickasaw Family

Willow's Adopted Family

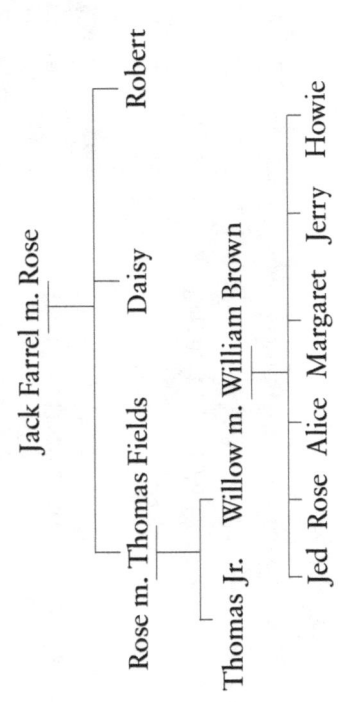

Jack Farrel m. Rose

Rose m. Thomas Fields   Daisy   Robert

Thomas Jr.   Willow m. William Brown

Jed Rose Alice Margaret Jerry Howie

Acknowledgments

I am grateful to Evan Pritchard, author, poet, teacher, friend, who pushed me to trust my imagination and listen to the ancestors. Thanks to my artist-daughter, Leola, for the cover drawing, and to my writer-daughter, Sandy, for editing. My brother, Sam, and sister, Torula, read drafts and made suggestions. Above all, I am thankful to my soul-mate husband, Paul, and grateful for our large community of friends in the Association of Native Americans of Mid-Hudson Valley, and in Neetopk Keetopk, as we strive to live in harmony with Earth.

If you loved *Willow's Secrets*, then you'll want to read
Indian Annie: A Grandmother's Story.